迷途之鸟

李 勇 - 译　　高 岩 - 译审

中国工人出版社

U0798319

contents

目录

译序

李勇

北京

2020.4

误读百年之后

今天为什么还要读泰戈尔

兼谈

我为什么翻译《迷途之鸟》

歌无垠，在天上
画无垠，在地上
诗无垠，在天地间
因为诗的词句中
有行走大地的意境
有翱翔天宇的音韵

——《迷途之鸟》第 204 首

这是印度一代诗圣泰戈尔对诗歌的诗化描述，他把诗歌看作众多艺术门类中一种可以沟通心灵与自然、幻化情感与世界、融通生命与永恒的天人合一的艺术形式。

泰戈尔其人

拉宾德拉纳特·泰戈尔（Rabindranath Tagore,1861—1941）是 20 世纪印度最伟大的诗人、文学家、艺术家。他 13 岁开始写诗，20 岁时因发表诗集《黄昏之歌》一举成名，一生创作了近 2000 首诗歌（50 部诗集）、100 余部小说、20 余部戏剧、近 2000 幅绘画以及不计其数的歌曲作品。此外，他还留下了有关文学、语言、哲学、宗教、政治、历史等方面的大量著述，包括评论、回忆录、游记、书简等。泰戈尔不仅是印度近代文学的奠基人和最高成就者，也是世界文明史上一位高山仰止的文化巨匠。

泰戈尔的名字在中国如雷贯耳，其作品很早就被介绍到中国，他也曾两次访问中国，他本人和他的作品都曾在中国掀起旋风，对中国新文学创作产生了极为深远的影响，一大批中国作家在文学创作上受到过泰戈尔风格的影响。

1924 年 5 月 12 日，诗人徐志摩在北京主持泰戈尔访华期间的一场重要演讲时，用充沛的情感、激越的语调和大量赞美之词，向中国青年讴歌、推介泰戈尔和他的作品，他把泰戈尔的人格、意志、想象力、创造力和艺术成就与惠特曼、托尔斯泰、米开朗基罗、歌德、苏格拉底、老聃等相提并论，呼吁青年学生爱他、崇拜他。

徐志摩说："他是三春和暖的南风，惊醒树枝上的新芽，增添处女颊上的红晕。他是普照的阳光。他是一派浩瀚的大水，来从不可追寻的渊源，在大地的怀抱中终古的流着，不息的流着，我们只是两岸的居民，凭借这慈恩的天赋，灌溉我们的田稻，苏解我们的消渴，洗净我们的污垢。他是喜马拉雅积雪的山峰，一般的崇高，一般的纯洁，一般的壮丽，一般的高傲，只有无限的青天枕藉他银白的头颅。"

徐志摩称泰戈尔是"自然界的一个神秘的现象"，"是不可侵凌的，不可逾越的"，他不愧是泰戈尔在中国最忠实的知音。

迷途之鸟的含义

对于这位极富传奇色彩的天才艺术创作家而言，诗歌仍是他最主要的成就。他的诗大部分用其母语孟加拉语写就，有时他也直接用英文写作，并亲自将自己的部分作品译成了英文。泰戈尔的诗因在普世价值的层面讴歌自然与人性之美，而被东西方文化广为接受，1913 年他荣膺诺贝尔文学奖，成为东方世界第一位获此殊荣的文学泰斗。

泰戈尔的著名诗集包括 *Gitanjali*（《吉檀迦利》）、*The Crescent Moon*（《新月集》）、*The Gardener*（《园丁集》）和 *Stray Birds*（《迷途之鸟》，或译为《飞鸟集》）。

《迷途之鸟》是泰戈尔在获得诺贝尔文学奖之后创作的一部诗集，是泰戈尔重要的代表作之一，也是他众多诗集中最有特色的一部。《迷途之鸟》因郑振铎先生最早将其翻译成《飞鸟集》，因而有了《飞鸟集》这个流传甚广的中文译名。Stray Birds 直译即为“迷途的鸟”，将之翻译成“飞鸟”显然是不准确的，为忠实原著，本人将此诗集译为《迷途之鸟》（此前也有部分译本使用了《迷途之鸟》的译名）。

《迷途之鸟》共计 325 首（序号编排为 326 首，但由于原作编辑疏忽，英文原版中第 263 首与第 98 首内容相同）。从形式上看，每首诗均无标题，字数精练，一般只有一两句话，且不押韵，因而有人将之归为散文诗；从内容上看，《迷途之鸟》多为哲理诗，是泰戈尔对世间万物和人生百态深情关注、深入洞察、深切感知、深刻感悟的成果和结晶，是他关于自然、宇宙，时间、生命，人生、命运的哲思集锦，这些包罗万象、色彩斑斓、芳香四溢、沁人心脾的哲思妙语处处闪烁着智慧的光芒和博爱的光辉，却以一种信马由缰、信手拈来的形式呈现出来，这恰是感性的文学作品与理性的哲学论述的区别所在。

诗集编排在整体上没有特定顺序和内在逻辑，但我发现，泰戈尔对第一首诗的安排是独具匠心的。“迷途之鸟”之名便取自第一首诗描绘的“夏日里迷途的鸟儿”，在我看来，这本诗集中每一缕清新的思绪，每一句精辟的话语，都像是一只只来去匆匆、天马行空的小鸟——我以为，这就是这本诗集取名为《迷途之鸟》的原因所在。所谓“迷途之鸟”指的就是这三百余首不拘一格、极简精妙、自由飞舞的小诗，所谓“迷途”就是不囿于固定格式和范式，不陷于僵化教条和路径的一种自由状态；就是偶然间“来到我的窗前”，“歌唱”然后又“飞离”的这份缘分和随性。

泰戈尔把这三百多首小诗比作迷途之鸟的歌唱和飘零落叶的叹息，在内容上具有强烈的象征意义，在形式上体现了碎片化的写作风格。因此，我认为《迷途之鸟》之译名更能准确体现作者的本意。

今天为什么还要读泰戈尔

我从很小的时候就开始读郑振铎和冰心翻译的泰戈尔诗歌，从中获得的心灵滋养令我受益终身。到了快知天命的时候，突然得到一大段闲暇，偏居一隅，冥思苦索，此时重读泰戈尔，如醍醐灌顶，茅塞顿开，悟到了几分人生的真谛。当今世界，各类文化和精神产品的表现形式可谓极其丰富，电影、音乐、戏剧、小说……而互联网和数字技术的发展又极大地拓展了多媒体艺术的表现方式，给人们带来前所未有的感官和娱乐的盛宴，在这样一个以视频和图像审美为特征的数字化时代，还有必要让年轻人去读诗歌，去读泰戈尔的诗歌吗？

答案是肯定的。因为文学是所有艺术形式中最基本的元素，离开了文学，人类就失去了叙事、表达和抒情的能力；离开了文学，就没有戏剧、电影、歌曲，甚至小品、曲艺；缺少了文学养分，所有的艺术形式都只会沦为廉价的文化快餐，而文化快餐的市场取向和媚俗冲动是难以遏制的。离开了文学，人类的精神世界就会出现营养不良或饥饿的症状。

以我在媒体行业工作二十多年的经验，我深知 3D、虚拟现实和人工智能技术的突飞猛进正在引发新一轮媒体革命，这必将给人们带来更逼真、更震撼、更具临场感和穿越感，即时性和互动性更强的视听体验。但也许正因为如此，我更加感受到了文学的力量，因为任何基于技术的艺术形式，无论其表现力和冲击力多么巨大，与无声的文学相比，也是有局限、有边界的，数字技术只能产生量化的艺术，而文学带给人们的细腻情感、心灵感动、巨大的思考和想象空间是不可限量的。文学只需寥寥数语，就可描绘万马奔腾、惊心动魄的场面；就可表达惊天动地、惊世骇俗的观点；就可传达直抵人心、震撼灵魂的感悟。更何况，文学的意境是任何具象的技术手段和计算机算法都无法破解和表现的。

恰恰是互联网时代，信息爆炸和娱乐泛滥更容易使人们迷失精神追求，丧失阅读、审美和独立思考的能力，因为以视频为主体的新媒体形式不能给人们留下足够的思考时间，面对强烈的视听冲击，人们往往是被动接受，极易导致审美过程的浅表化，进而导致审美判断和审美经验的缺失。而只有文学、绘画、雕塑、音乐这些最原始的艺术形式才可以使欣赏者凝神观照、聚精思考、浮想联翩……从而激发人的想象力，培养人的高尚情感和审美情趣。

如果远离文学，任由感官刺激替代精神享受，文化快餐和快餐文化麻痹审美神经，那么人们在生活更加富裕、享受到更多物质快乐的同时，却无法享受到渗透了崇高精神、真挚情感和文明积淀的心灵上的快乐。

文学是人类最古老的精神家园，人类无论发展到什么阶段，都离不开文学艺术的滋养，数字媒体时代，青年人更应该通读文学经典，感受绘画、雕塑和音乐的魅力，以避免审美能力的丧失，避免生活的庸俗化和情趣的肤浅化。

泰戈尔的诗歌里并没有什么复杂难懂的词语，他描绘和讴歌的都是小草、白云、高山、大海、河流、瀑布、太阳、星辰等这些大自然中的平凡而美丽的事物，他的语句和结构也不像后现代主义诗歌那样晦涩抽象，但他诗中的意境和幻象，以及其中蕴含的深意却不是每一个人都能轻易读懂的，郑振铎称之“包含着深邃的大道理”，这恰是泰戈尔的博大精深之处，也是泰戈尔诗歌的魅力所在。

●●●　●●●

今晨，我坐在窗前
世界犹如一位过客
在我面前驻足片刻
向我示意
然后离开

——《迷途之鸟》第 16 首

你看不到自己
你看到的是你的影子

——《迷途之鸟》第 18 首

在第 16 首中，诗人把世界放在一个客体的位置，把世界当作一个与“我”平等的人，他给我们提供了一种何等豁达和傲然的观察世界的视角；而在第 18 首中，诗人又告诉我们应该如何看待和认识自己，你是谁？你能认清这个世界和你自己吗？

瀑布唱道：
唯有自由
令我放歌

——《迷途之鸟》第 36 首

只有最渴望自由和最热爱自由的人才能洞悉瀑布飞流直下时的壮观豪情，才能领略到自由的巨大势能和力量。

伐木的斧头向树
索求一根木柄
树成全了它

——《迷途之鸟》第 71 首

树是愚钝的，还是宽容的？斧头是凶狠的，还是可怜的？诗人寥寥数笔，描绘了两个鲜明的形象，一段精彩的对话、一则精妙的寓言。

“你是荷叶下面的一颗大露珠，
我是荷叶上面的一颗小露珠。”
露珠对湖水如是说。

——《迷途之鸟》第 88 首

是不是与老庄“梦莲”有异曲同工之妙？大与小的相对性、梦与被梦的相对性都体现了独特的东方哲学智慧。

理解诗，需要读者调动自身的想象力，需要读者参与到诗人的创作过程之中去，需要读者与诗人心灵之间的感应与共振。诗人虽然不在了，但他的诗句仍然鲜活地存在着，我们读李白、苏东坡是如此，读徐志摩和余光中是如此，读泰戈尔也是如此。我相信，每一个人心中都有一个自己的泰戈尔。在泰戈尔的诗中，你可以读到天地之纯净、自然之宽厚、生命之绚烂、岁月之芬芳、死亡之静美。

百年翻译之怪现状

每个人对泰戈尔的理解都可以不同，但翻译的基本要求是尽可能保留原文的含义。

个人认为，目前国内有关泰戈尔的诗作翻译主要存在的问题，大致有如下几类。

一、恶搞。

此类行为出版界已有批评，借亵渎经典来表现自己是一种极不道德的行为，此处不予赘述。

二、原文抄录错误。

如第 8 首原文：“Her wistful face haunts my dreams like the rain at night”。不少中译本把 wistful 抄成了 wishful，翻译结果当然不同。

再如第 123 首：“The bird thinks it is an act of kindness to give the fish a lift in the air”。不少版本把 lift 误抄为 life，于是有了“鸟儿认为让鱼在空中生活是一种善行 / 鸟儿以为能在空中给鱼儿一条性命就是善举一桩”这样的译文，原文的意思是鸟儿以自己的思维和行为模式去行善，却忽略了鱼儿的需求，而 give a lift 恰是鸟儿的一种行为动作，因此我译为：

鸟儿以为
它把鱼儿叼出水面是一个善举

因在选择原著版本时缺乏严谨的态度，甚至根本未进行基本的辨识，难免以讹传讹。

三、望文生义。

比如第7首：“The sands in your way beg for your song and your movement,dancing water.Will you carry the burden of their lameness?”。大多数版本把 movement 译成运动，或流动、律动，因而有了“……请求你的歌声和你的流动”这样的翻译，原意实为期待与流水一起走，这样才有后面的一句问话：“Will you carry the burden of their lameness?”，因此我译成：乞求随你的歌声同行。化解名词 movement。

舞动的流水啊

你途中的沙子乞求随你的歌声同行
你愿意背负这些跛脚的沙吗

第36首，多数译者翻译成：“瀑布唱道：当我发现自由的时候，也发现了歌”。其实，when 在这里不是时间连词，是条件连词，表达一种特定条件下才会产生的状态。因此，我的翻译是：

瀑布唱道：
唯有自由
令我放歌

再如第 122 首，有人翻译成：“亲爱的朋友，我聆听海涛时，就能感受到你对这片海滨上无数深沉的黄昏，正在进行伟大的冥想。”之所以有“对海滨的黄昏进行冥想”这样的翻译，是因为译者把“of many a deepening eventide on this beach”中的 of 当作了从属介词，其实这个小小的 of 在此是英文的一个旧用法，表示时间，即在黄昏思考，而非思考黄昏。我的译文是：

亲爱的朋友
多少个深沉的黄昏
在这个岸边听涛声响起
我领悟到你伟大思想的静寂

● ● ● ● ● ●

第 230 首，有版本译作：“让放眼看玫瑰的人只看刺”，还有“让睁眼看到玫瑰花的人也看到它的刺”。这些都是典型的硬翻，只读中文的读者一定莫名其妙。我的翻译是：

让喜爱玫瑰的人
留意一下她的刺

第 214 首，绝大多数版本把“lends the colours of the rainbow to”译成“把彩虹的颜色借给……”，如：我们的欲望把彩虹的颜色借给纯属云雾的人生。中文读者对“借颜色”一定莫名其妙，其实 lend colour to sth 是英文中的一个固定用法，根据《牛津高阶英汉双解词典》的解释，它的意思是“使显得真实（或可能）”，如 lend your name to sth 的意思是“公开表示支持”，岂能译成“借名字”？“lend support, weight, credence, etc. to sth”都是类似用法，翻译时无须也不能把“借”字翻出来。因此，我的翻译是：

有了渴盼
原本虚无缥缈的人生
就会变得如彩虹般真实绚烂

再如第 233 首原文：“In heart’s perspective the distance looms large”。有人译为：“在心的远景里，距离赫然显得大起来”；也有人译为：“在心的远景里，距离隐约变得更远了”。其实，loom large 也是一个英语惯用语，不能逐字硬翻，《牛津高阶英汉双解词典》中释义为：“令人忧虑，令人惊恐（并似乎难以避免）”。而 perspective 在此也非景观、远景的意思，而是与态度、观点、判断力相关的含义。我的翻译是：

由心观之，疏远令人忧虑

诗集中多处出现 the other world 一词，多数版本翻译成：“另一个世界、其他的世界”，其实，the other world 是与 the world“此世、现世”相对应的“彼世、来世”。

四、曲解原意。

如第 34 首："The dry river-bed finds no thanks for its past"。有人译作："枯竭的河床，对自己往事的感激之情难以言表"。find no thanks 是"认为不必感谢，不归功于……"的意思，诗歌原意与"找不到感谢的字眼""感激之情难以言表"南辕北辙。我的翻译是：

干涸的河床
毫不感激自己的过去

第 62 首："The Perfect decks itself in beauty for the love of the Imperfect"是一句寓意深刻的经典哲理诗，完美和不完美是相对的，是可以相互转化的，正是"不完美"的存在才造就了"完美"。我的翻译是：

出于对"不完美"的爱
"完美"扮靓自己

而这样的翻译："完美为了向缺陷示爱，把自己打扮得花枝招展"，把"不完美"译成"缺陷"完全破坏了原作设置的 Perfect 和 Imperfect 之间的对比关系和逻辑内涵，而把 in beauty 译成"花枝招展"，纯属过度翻译。

有译本把第 82 首：“Let life be beautiful like summer flowers and death like autumn leaves”翻译成：“让生如夏花般美艳，死如秋叶”。这句诗的经典翻译出自郑振铎之手：“使生如夏花之绚烂，死如秋叶之静美”。这已是流传几十年的名句。但译者却坚决不把秋叶的美翻译出来，并在其“译注”中解释说：“这首诗前半截强调美，一目了然。但后半截强调什么，诗人没有明说，只说如秋叶。夏花的特性比较简单，甚至可以说单一，那就是美丽，这是无可争议的，因此诗人可以把生比喻成夏花的美丽，意思清晰明了。但是对死虽然以秋叶来比喻，但并未说出像秋叶的什么特征。”针对郑振铎先生的译文，这位译者提出强烈质疑，认为郑译是“想当然的发挥，虽然很美，但失当”，“秋叶看上去的确很美，但死亡却没有什么美可谈。因为无论如何死去，死亡对生命来说都是可怕的”。

其实，从英文语法角度看，后半句显然是“and death be beautiful like autumn leaves”省略了 be beautiful，因此泰戈尔原意就是把死比作美的，夏花的美只是铺垫，死亡之美才是泰戈尔想告诉我们的，郑译恰到好处，并未过度发挥。

拒绝把死比作美，这已完全不是翻译的问题，而是文化和哲学观念上的差异了。东西方很多哲学思想，包括基督教在内的许多宗教都认为生与死都是自然过程中的一部分，都是美的。老子说，“反者道之动”，道本身就包含着它的对立面非道、反道，有生就有死，生死一体；庄子也认为，自然本身就包含着反自然的元素，生与死是一回事，“孰能以无为首，以生为脊，以死为尻，孰知死生存亡之一体者，吾与之友矣”。

泰戈尔在这本诗集第 268 首中吟道：

生与死都是生命题中应有之义
如抬步、落步都属于行走一样

诗人在第 313 首中说：

总有一天，我们会明白
死亡永远不会掠走我们灵魂的收获
因为灵魂的收获就是灵魂本身

再读读第 316 首：

主啊，让我真实地活着
那样，死亡对我也就变得真实了

任何事物都是矛盾对立的统一体，没有死亡也就没有生命。然而，今天的中国人普遍缺少生死观教育，确有不少中国人把死看作可怕的、不吉利的事物。难怪一些中国人在欧美或日本见到人家把先人的墓碑立于繁华地段或自家庭院的显赫位置，而大惊小怪。“死亡却没有什么美可谈”与“好死不如赖活着”属于同一认知水准，却与泰戈尔思想的高深境界相去甚远。

再如第 92 首，这样的译文实在不知所云：“叶的生死乃是涡流的急骤旋转，但它更加宽阔的轨道在繁星间却运转迟缓”。

其实，这句诗反映了诗人把具象与抽象、宏观和微观统合对比的强大想象力，泰戈尔把树叶的生死轮回比作一个漩涡（圆圈），而这个漩涡的外圈（更宽阔的一些圆圈）就是天体运行的轨道，这与第 88 首“荷叶上下的露珠”之表达有异曲同工之妙，表达的是万物归一、天人合一的哲学思想。我的翻译是：

树叶的生死轮回犹如快速旋转的漩涡
而漩涡的外圈是天体缓慢运行的轨道

第 215 首：“God waits to win back his own flowers as gifts from man’s hands”有人译为：“神等待着，要把自己的花儿作为礼物，从人们的手中夺回”。这个译文真是对上

帝仁慈之心的歪曲。此句的本意是上帝希望人有感恩之心，懂得回馈上天的恩赐。为了把意思说透，我在翻译时适当添加了几个字词：

上帝想从人的手里赢回自己的鲜花
他等待人将之作为礼物回赠他

第 323 首："I have suffered and despaired and known death and I am glad that I am in this great world"有人翻译为："我经历磨难，已然绝望，对死亡了如指掌；我与这个伟大世界同在，我为此心花怒放"。know 译成"了如指掌"，glad 译成"心花怒放"，这些过度翻译违背原意。我的翻译是：

经历了苦难
经历了绝望
懂得了死亡
我庆幸我生活在
这个伟大的世界

五、追求不必要的押韵。

很多译者误以为诗歌必须押韵。殊不知，诗歌是形式最为多样的文学样式，固然诗歌有韵律、格律、音调、节奏等方面的约束，但形式是为内容服务的，新诗被称作自由诗，后现代主义诗歌在表达方式上更是无拘无束、放荡不羁。押韵并不等于就是美，为押韵而押韵有时反而破坏了诗歌的意境，沦为打油诗、顺口溜。外国诗歌的翻译更不该追求押韵，因为无论原作是否押韵，翻译过来都无法保留原文的韵律，所以追求中文译文的押韵是毫无意义的。特别是《迷途之鸟》，原文本就不押韵，译文为何一定要押韵呢？有些译本刻意追求押韵，有时不得不人为破坏了原文的意义，有时又不可避免地陷入一种语言游戏的滑稽状态，这样的“再创作”是得不偿失的。

翻译的错误和缺陷，与其说是翻译者外语水平的局限造成的，不如说是翻译者对原著理解的局限造成的，是翻译者文学功底、背景知识、哲思水平，甚至中文表达能力的不足所致。

百年误读之遗憾

我一向认为，诗是不可以翻译的。因为诗是无声的音乐，它对韵律、节奏的追求和把握，对词汇、短语的选择和搭配是高度依赖某一种特定语言的，是依赖这种特定语言的独特特征而创作的，无论把唐诗宋词译成英文还是把雪莱、歌德的作品译成中文，语言的鸿沟都无法填平，诗歌的美艳和意境都荡然无存了。

诗歌与小说、散文等体裁不同，它不以叙事见长，不以纯粹的情节描述、人物刻画、情景描写为内容，它的目的不是把某件事情说清楚，反而力图消解惯常的逻辑，力图破坏表层的语法，它追求的是一种意向、一种意境、一种深入潜意识的真实和真诚、一种触及灵魂的理解与共鸣。诗歌大量运用隐喻、暗喻、抽象、象征、潜台词、意识流等手段，来表达思想和情感，它在修辞上常常有意出格，甚至违背一般的写作律条。无论风格豪放或细腻，诗人都强烈追求夸张、对比等出人意料的艺术效果，给人带来视觉、听觉、情感和思想上的剧烈冲击以及无穷的遐想与回味，以此启迪智慧，打动人心。

此外，诗人常常不以主体的表达或客体的陈述为手段，诗歌创作是诗人极其隐秘的心灵活动，真正的诗人在创作的时候不会像某些纪实类或小说类作者那样考虑市场需求，甚至迎合市场口味，也就是说诗人写作时一般不会考虑读者或受众的感受，不会考虑读者是否能看懂。难怪经常有人抱怨，诗歌“读不懂”，即便是同文的读者，如果没有一定的文学修养，也是读不懂的，何况透过翻译去读诗呢？所以，一位美国诗人曾说，一首诗中能够翻译过来的，仅仅是原诗中非诗的那部分。这是一个事实。

其实，即便是以故事讲述为主体的小说，要翻译到位、传神也是很难的。日本大作家村上春树，曾翻译过美国小说家斯科特·菲兹杰拉德的名著《了不起的盖茨比》，以下是村上春树翻译这本小说时的感慨：

《了不起的盖茨比》的作者斯科特·菲兹杰拉德28岁时文笔达到巅峰。然而翻译成日语之后，无论是否出于译者本意，都会有很多美妙之处受到损伤。就如同上好的葡萄酒经过长途运输一样，独特的芳香和微妙的口感难免会有损失。

所以，很容易形成这样的看法：这种小说阅读原文是最佳选择。然而阅读原文又非普通读者能够实现的。空气的微妙流动，使得相应的色调、情形和节奏每时每刻都在变化，这种自由自在、畅通无阻的美丽文体，没有相当的阅读水准的确很难体会到。从某种程度上说，并不是懂英语就能领略到这种等级的叙事美感。

因此，说得夸张一点，《了不起的盖茨比》至今没有被日本大部分读者真正正确地认识。……这其中的原因恐怕很大程度上就是翻译存在着局限。

……

作为一个翻译者，作为一个小说家，我会尽我的努力和诚意寻找一条翻译之路，将《了不起的盖茨比》这部作品最重要、最本质的东西，尽可能有效而准确地表达出来。[注]

村上春树的上述描述与我对泰戈尔作品在中国命运的感觉如出一辙，虽然泰戈尔在中国影响很大，但广大中文版读者对其作品所拥有的超越自然的神性是低估的，就连一些翻译者自己也未能读到泰戈尔的真谛。例如，一位翻译者在其译作序言中说他在翻译《迷途之鸟》中悟出了强烈的环保意识，他说："泰戈尔的杰作便令每一位读者对环保形势生发出深深的忧患意识。"尽管泰戈尔的诗中充满了花、草、蓝天、大海等字眼，但如果我们不能从哲学和艺术的层面去认识和理解泰戈尔的作品，无论使用什么样的溢美之词，都是对泰戈尔深邃思想和巨大成就的一种贬低。

其实，对泰戈尔作品中文翻译的争议已存在了快一个世纪了。《迷途之鸟》最早的中译本《飞鸟集》是由郑振铎于1922年翻译出版的。这个译本虽然只是郑振铎的选译本，但对向中国读者介绍泰戈尔及其作品，发挥了重要的启蒙作用。但是这个译本甫一出版，即遭到了梁实秋、成仿吾等人的尖锐批评，成为文坛一段公案。梁实秋写道："我只是校了郑

注　摘自村上春树的文章《身为翻译者，身为小说家》，收录于《了不起的盖茨比》中译本（南海出版公司，2013年9月）。

译的前十首，一共发现了四个错误，我实在再没耐心校下去了。”郑振铎的译本确有不少错误，他回应批评者说：“我有一大毛病，就是做事太粗心。常常在急待付印之时，才着手去做或译稿子，永远不会再读再校一次的，因此常常出现了许多不必出现的错误。”当时，郑振铎还是二十几岁的青年，翻译受到思想和阅历的局限是一件正常的事。不正常的是，快一个世纪过去了，在资讯如此发达的互联网时代，我们仍然无法准确破译泰戈尔，读不懂他留下的文字。

翻译的错误，大大降低了泰戈尔作品的意涵，使其中译本沦为廉价的心灵鸡汤，这不能不说是泰戈尔作品在中国的一大憾事。

我为什么要翻译《迷途之鸟》

虽然很多人都认同“诗是不可以翻译的”，但伟大的诗歌是必须翻译的，因为它们是全人类的文化遗产，必须得到有力的跨文化传播。一个人不可能通晓所有的语言，但一个具备基本文学素养的人不可能不读雪莱、拜伦、叶芝和歌德，这就是翻译者的责任。

目睹泰戈尔作品在中国被误读百年之怪现状，作为一名泰戈尔诗歌的拥趸和一位诗歌创作者，我决定翻译泰戈尔的代表作 Stray Birds，向中国读者，特别是青年人，介绍真正的泰戈尔。我的目的是让中文读者尽可能地了解泰戈尔作品的原貌，领悟他所描绘的哲思境界。翻译过程中，我始终坚持以下几个原则。

首先，忠实于原著，保持原作风貌。一是不改其本意，尽可能完整准确地表达原作的内容；二是不删繁就简，不添枝加叶，尽可能保持原作的文风，避免简化翻译和过度翻译，避免自以为是的“再创作”。

其次，忠实展现原作的艺术内涵。诗歌最美之处在于诗人超越常人思维的独特创意，因此翻译过程中要尽可能将作者的创意挖掘出来，表现出来，译文不得淹没原作的智慧，要让作者的创作意图尽可能地到达译文读者的心中。

再次，追求译文本身的美感。外国诗歌译本总给人艰深晦涩、不知所云的印象，这主要是逐字逐句机械直译、硬译造成的，中外文语法规则不同，译文应尽可能符合中文阅读习惯，译文本身也应具备诗歌的形式美感。毋庸讳言，翻译是一项再创作，再创作的本质不是在内容上进行发挥，而是选择最佳的中文表达方式，以尽可能展现原作之美。

这三个原则与老一代翻译家概括的“信、达、雅”三个境界是一致的，我希望向大家提供一个尽可能完善的译本。

我发现我在这篇文章中使用了太多“尽可能”这个词，因为就翻译这项工作而言，完美是一个永远不可能达到的目标。本书比较了国外多家出版公司的多个经典版本以确保英文原文的准确无误，同时按照中英文对照的方式编排，希望有一定英文水平的读者在阅读过程中能够尽可能地去接触原文，体验不同语言和文化相互碰撞迸发出的魅力。

关于《星迹》

在这个译本编辑出版的过程中，我的挚友、我最敬佩的中国当代艺术家——董小庄先生为这本诗集无偿奉献了一批珍贵而至美的艺术佳作。董小庄说：“做好一件事情真不容易，诞生一幅优秀的艺术作品更难，聚集一批艺术大师整体性创作不仅仅是一种挑战了！”

2016年，小庄先生邀请当今世界最优秀的十二位艺术家用各自不同的艺术手法共同完成以“十二星座”为表现对象的艺术创作，这是继“艺会五洲”之后，小庄先生策划、运作的又一个全球性的艺术家跨文化创作体验活动，是当代国际艺术交流领域的又一大壮举。

经过五年艰辛努力，终于有了本书收录的这十二位艺术大师的144幅同题绘画作品（每人12幅），小庄先生将这个作品系列命名为《星迹》。《星迹》是来自东西方不同文化背景的艺术家对宇宙和星空、对时空和命运的不同诠释。这些艺术佳作让我们看到，即便面对同一个主题、同一件事物，不同艺术家的表现方式也是截然不同的。个性是艺术的生命，独特性是艺术风格的价值所在。

《星迹》的表现内容与泰戈尔的诗歌有异曲同工之妙，让我们在对星空的仰望和对命运的遐想中领略不同思想流派、不同艺术风格交融、摩擦产生的绚丽火焰；领略文明多样性和艺术多元化的蓬勃生机。

泰戈尔的诗历经百年而生生不息，将这 144 幅美术作品与泰戈尔的诗完美组合，展现了不同艺术门类跨越地域、跨越时代、跨越一切天然与人造的鸿沟，共振共鸣的永恒之美。

因此，这是一本十分独特的书。

她集世界的万千美好于一身。

这种美，美得令人窒息。

为了这本书，为了这份美，我要特别感谢董小庄先生的慷慨支持；感谢十二位艺术大师的精彩呈现；感谢张今亮先生的独特编排和卓越设计。

谈及泰戈尔，徐志摩说：“我想只要我们的良心不曾受恶毒的烟煤熏黑，或是被恶浊的偏见污抹，谁不曾感觉他至诚的力量，魔术似的，为我们生命的前途开辟了一个神奇的境界，燃点了理想的光明？”

艺术的终极价值就是让人们即便是在至暗的时刻仍能感受到光明的希冀。期待徐志摩先生酣畅而激越的声音在近一个世纪之后，仍然能被今天的青年人听到，希望今天的中国青年也能认识泰戈尔、热爱泰戈尔、崇拜泰戈尔。这样，每一个中国人的心中就会拥有一汪澄澈的湖水。

St
Bi
The clouds fill the
hiding themselv

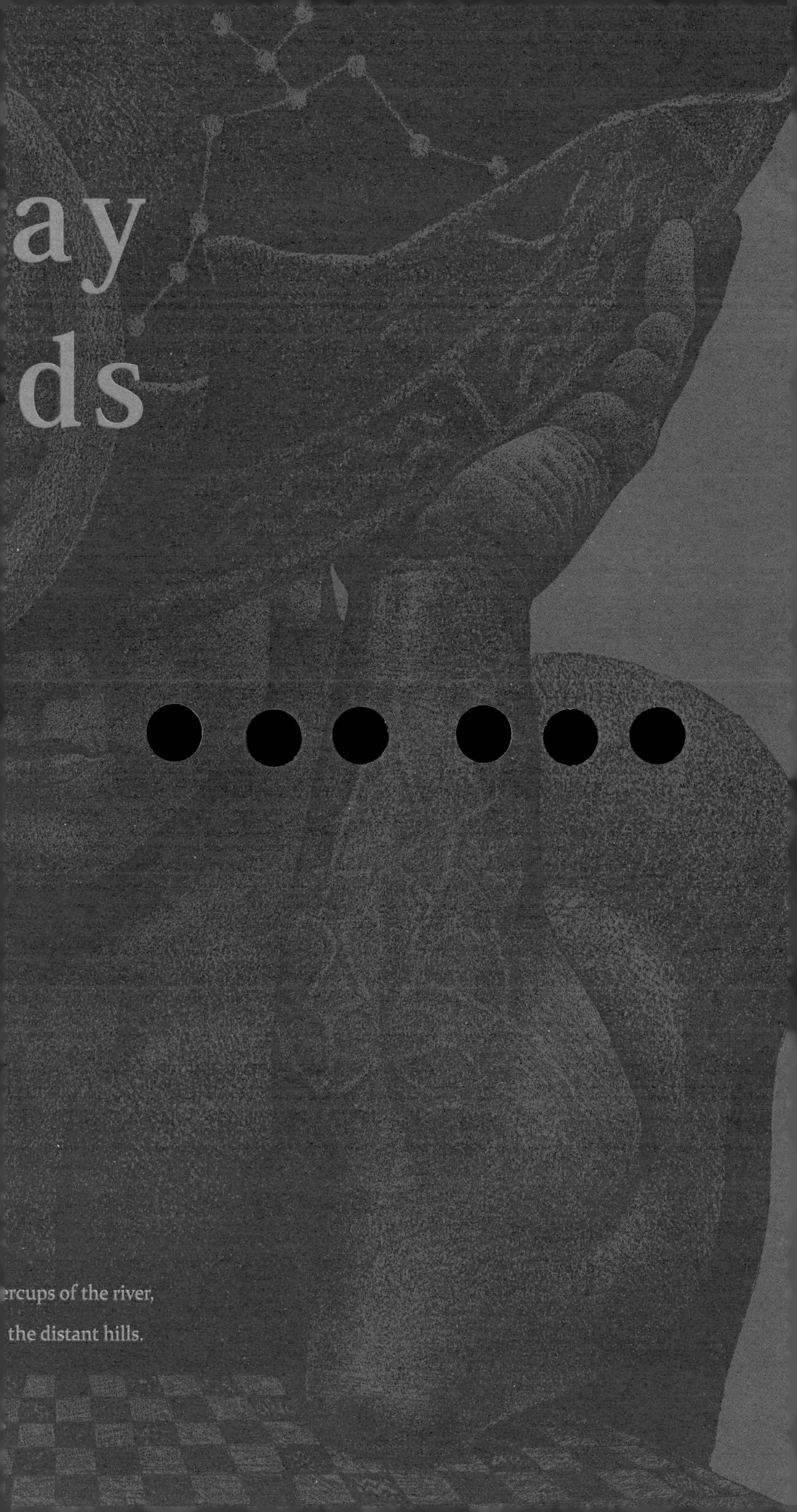

ay

ds

ercups of the river,

the distant hills.

Stray birds o

summer com

to my window t

sing and fly awa

And yellow leave

of autumn, whic

have no song

flutter and fa

there with a sig

Stray birds of summer come to my
window to sing and fly away.
And yellow leaves of autumn,
which have no songs, flutter and
fall there with a sigh.

白羊座 / Aries

夏日里迷途的鸟儿

来到我的窗前

歌唱

飞离

秋日里枯黄的落叶

无声地振翅

飘落

叹息

金牛座 / Taurus

002

O troupe of little vagrants
of the world, leave your
footprints in my words.

003

The world puts off its mask of
vastness to its lover.
It becomes small as one song, as
one kiss of the eternal.

哦，尘世上这帮渺小的流浪者
把你们的足迹留在我的文字里吧

世界在它的爱人面前摘下面具
不再广袤
它变得如此渺小
如一支歌
如永恒之吻

004

It is the tears of the earth that

keep her smiles in bloom.

005

The mighty desert is burning

for the love of a blade of grass

who shakes her head and

laughs and flies away.

是大地的泪水

让她的笑容盛开

浩瀚的沙漠

因爱着一叶绿草

而燃烧

那小草

却摇摇头

笑着

飞走了

006

If you shed tears when you miss the sun, you also miss the stars.

双子座 / Gemini

如果你因为错过了太阳而落泪

那么，你也会错过群星

巨蟹座 / Cancer

007

The sands in your way beg for your song
and your movement, dancing water.
Will you carry the burden of their
lameness?

008

Her wistful face haunts
my dreams like the rain
at night.

舞动的流水啊

你途中的沙子乞求随你的歌声同行

你愿意背负这些跛脚的沙吗

她伤感的面容

如夜雨一般

萦绕着我的梦

009

Once we dreamt that we were strangers.
We wake up to find that we were dear to each other.

010

Sorrow is hushed into peace in my heart like the evening among the silent trees.

梦中，我们曾形同陌路
醒来，才发现彼此亲昵

悲伤在我的心中归于平静
犹如夜幕降于寂静的树林

011

Some unseen fingers, like an idle breeze, are playing upon my heart the music of the ripples.

狮子座 / Leo

看不见的手指
如慵懒的微风
拨弄我的心弦
乐音迤逦

处女座 / Virgo

012

"What language is thine, O sea?"

"The language of eternal question."

"What language is thy answer, O sky?"

"The language of eternal silence."

013

Listen, my heart, to the whispers

of the world with which it makes

love to you.

“大海啊，你说的是哪一种语言？”

“我的语言是永恒的提问。”

“天空啊，你用哪一种语言回答它呢？”

“我的语言是永恒的沉默。”

听啊，我的心

这个世界的低语

正是对你的示爱

014

The mystery of creation is like the darkness of night— it is great. Delusions of knowledge are like the fog of the morning.

015

Do not seat your love upon a precipice because it is high.

创造的神秘如夜的黑暗

——如此伟岸

而知识的幻象

如同晨间的迷雾

勿将你的爱置于悬崖峭壁

因为那里太险峻

I sit at my window this morning
where the world like a passer-by
stops for a moment, nods to me and
goes.

天秤座 / Libra

今晨，我坐在窗前

世界犹如一位过客

在我面前驻足片刻

向我示意

然后离开

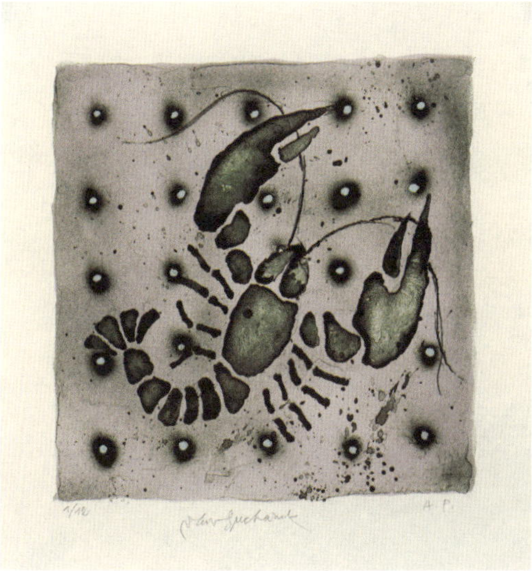

天蝎座 / Scorpio

017

These little thoughts are the rustle of leaves; they have their whisper of joy in my mind.

018

What you are you do not see, what you see is your shadow.

缕缕思绪如树叶窸窣

在我心中欢乐地低语

你看不到你自己

你看到的是你的影子

019

My wishes are fools, they shout
across thy songs, my Master.
Let me but listen.

020

I cannot choose the best.
The best chooses me.

我的主啊
我的愿望如此愚蠢
竟向你的歌声叫嚣
且容我聆听吧

我不能选择最好的
总是最好的选择我

021

They throw their shadows before them who carry their lantern on their back.

022

That I exist is a perpetual surprise which is life.

把灯提在背后的人
在自己面前布下阴影

我的存在是一个持续不断的惊奇
——这就是生活

023

"We, the rustling leaves, have a voice that answers the storms,but who are you so silent?"

"I am a mere flower."

射手座 / Sagittarius

“我们——树叶，用窸窣的声音回应风暴。

可你是谁呀，如此沉默？”

“我只是一朵花。”

摩羯座 / Capricorn

024

Rest belongs to the work as the eyelids to the eyes.

025

Man is a born child, his power is the power of growth.

休憩服从于工作
恰如眼睑听命于眼睛

人类天生就是孩子
他的力量在于成长

026

God expects answers for the flowers he sends us, not for the sun and the earth.

027

The light that plays, like a naked child, among the green leaves happily knows not that man can lie.

上帝期待回报

——对他送给我们的鲜花

而非他送给我们的太阳和地球

光像一个赤裸的孩子

在绿叶间快乐地玩耍

他浑然不知人会说谎

028

O Beauty, find thyself in love, not in the flattery of thy mirror.

029

My heart beats her waves at the shore of the world and writes upon it her signature in tears with the words,“I love thee.”

啊，美人
在爱中发现你的美吧
切莫相信镜子的谄媚

我的心在世界的岸边激起波澜
然后用泪水在岸上写下这几个字的
印记——
“我爱你。”

030

“Moon, for what do you wait?”

“To salute the sun for whom I

must make way.”

水瓶座 / Aquarius

“月亮，你在等什么？ ”

“我等着给太阳敬个礼，

因为我得给他让路了。”

双鱼座 / Pisces

031

The trees come up to my window
like the yearning voice of the
dumb earth.

032

His own mornings are new
surprises to God.

树伸向我的窗子

犹如沉默的大地发出的

欲望之声

上帝对自己创造的每一个清晨

都充满新的惊喜

033

Life finds its wealth by the claims of the world, and its worth by the claims of love.

034

The dry river-bed finds no thanks for its past.

世俗的求索可以实现生活的富足
对爱的追求方能实现生命的价值

干涸的河床
毫不感激自己的过去

几个世纪以来，星座一直都是伟大的艺术灵感。让我的版画赋予每个星座一种当代感是我的创作目标。

弗拉迪米尔 · 苏哈尼克

Zodiac has been a great artistic inspiration for centuries. The goal of my graphic work is to give each of its signs a contemporary face.

Vladimir Suchanek

弗拉迪米尔·苏哈尼克 Vladimir Suchanek 捷克版画艺术家协会主席，欧洲科学艺术院院士，捷克国家艺术贡献奖获得者。1933 年生于捷克梅图耶河畔新城。1952 年至 1954 年在布拉格查理大学学习，师从布达教授、利迪基教授和萨尔克曼教授。1954 年至 1960 年在布拉格美术学院学习版画艺术，师从西洛夫斯基教授。1995 年至 2015 年任捷克版画艺术家协会主席。1997 年被欧洲科学艺术院授予院士称号。2006 年被授予捷克国家艺术贡献奖。擅长于版画、绘画及插画、邮票、书籍和藏书票设计。他在 20 世纪对欧洲及捷克石版画与技术的推动，使石版画艺术在国际具有广泛的影响力和领导作用。他在国际上赢得了 31 个至高的荣誉。2003 年在北京的国际版画双年展上获得了最高奖项。至 2018 年，在捷克和世界各地举办了 170 余场个人展览，参加 300 多场联展，如荷兰、比利时、德国、日本、美国、中国、瑞典、丹麦、希腊、波兰和斯洛伐克等。作品被众多国家博物馆、美术馆等重要艺术机构收藏。

Zodiak je po staletí velkou uměleckou inspirací.
Cílem mé grafické tvorby je dát každému z jeho znamení současnou tvář.

Vlad Suchánek

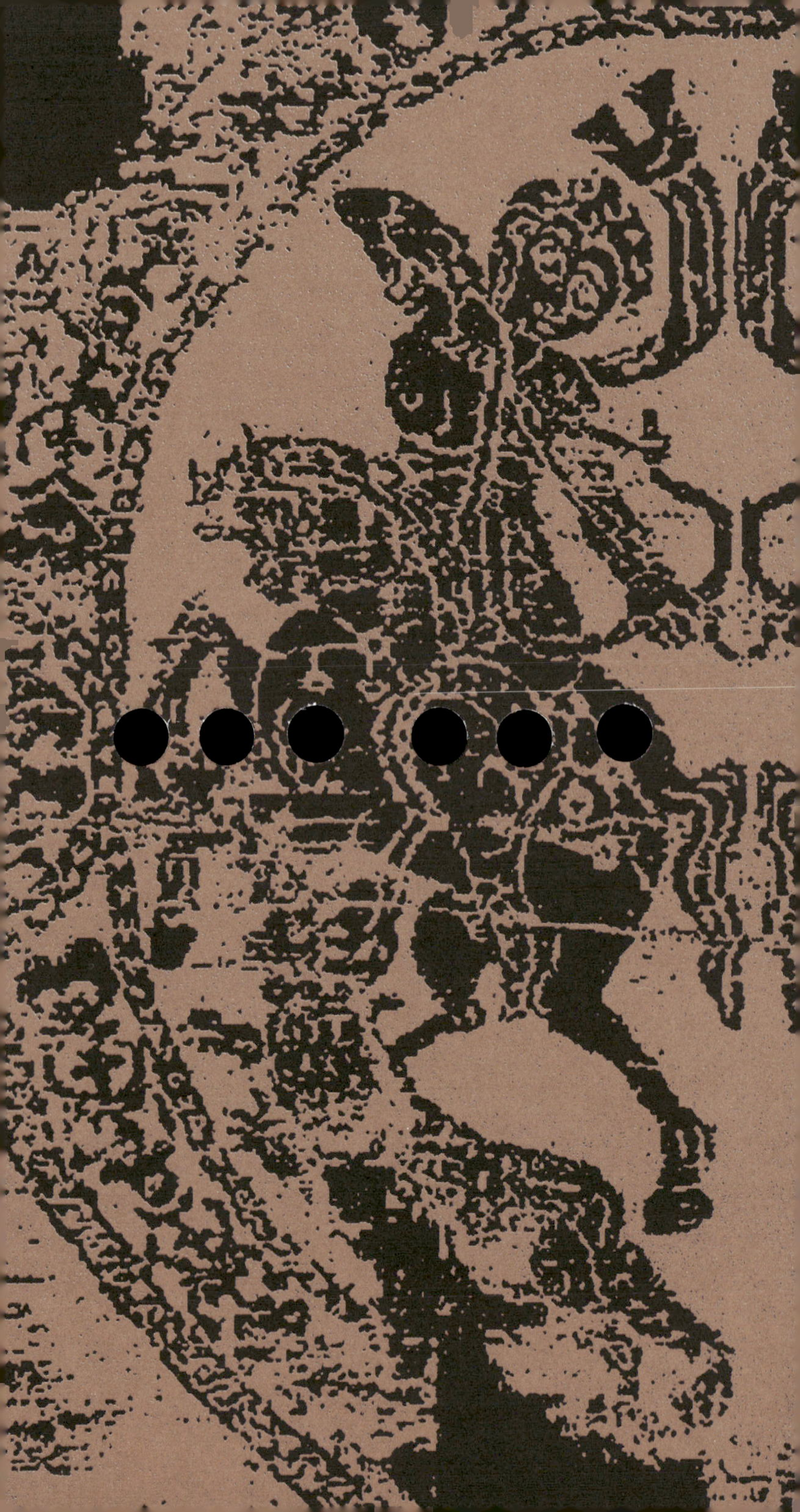

The fish in the wat

is silent, the anim

on the earth is nois

the bird in the air

singin

But Man has in him th

silence of the sea, th

noise of the earth ar

the music of the a

035

The bird wishes it were a cloud. The cloud wishes it were a bird.

白羊座 / Aries

鸟愿作一朵云

云愿为一只鸟

金牛座 / Taurus

036

The waterfall sings, "I find my song,
when I find my freedom."

037

I cannot tell why this heart
languishes in silence.
It is for small needs it never asks,
or knows or remembers.

瀑布唱道：

唯有自由

令我放歌

我真不明白

这颗心为何总在沉默中煎熬

为了那些

从未提出

或从未知晓

或从未记住的

微不足道的需要

Woman, when you move about in your household service your limbs sing like a hill stream among its pebbles.

双子座 / Gemini

女人，当你忙着操持家务时
你的肢体在歌唱，宛如
一股山泉在鹅卵石之间流淌

巨蟹座 / Cancer

039

The sun goes to cross the Western sea,

leaving its last salutation to the East.

040

Do not blame your food because

you have no appetite.

日落西海

挥别东方

没有胃口

别怪食物

041

The trees, like the longings of the earth, stand a-tiptoe to peep at the heaven.

狮子座 / Leo

树，如大地的渴望

踮着脚尖窥视天堂

处女座 / Virgo

042

You smiled and talked to me of nothing and I felt that for this I had been waiting long.

043

The fish in the water is silent, the animal on the earth is noisy, the bird in the air is singing.
But Man has in him the silence of the sea, the noise of the earth and the music of the air.

旷日的等待

等来的是你一语不发的微笑

水中的鱼静默

地上的兽喧闹

天上的鸟歌唱

而人却兼有

海的沉默

地的喧嚣

天的乐音

044

The world rushes on over the strings of the lingering heart making the music of sadness.

045

He has made his weapons his gods. When his weapons win he is defeated himself.

世界拨弄着彷徨的心弦

奏出悲伤的乐曲

他拜手中的武器为神

武器获胜时，他败给了自己

046

God finds himself by creating.

天秤座 / Libra

造物主在创造中自得

天蝎座 / Scorpio

047

Shadow, with her veil drawn, follows Light in secret meekness, with her silent steps of love.

048

The stars are not afraid to appear like fireflies.

影子

披上她的面纱

隐秘地

温顺地

拖着无声的

爱的脚步

追随

光

星星并不惧怕

形似萤火虫

049

I thank thee that I am none of the wheels of power but I am one with the living creatures that are crushed by it.

射手座 / Sagittarius

谢天谢地，我非强权之轮

而是被其碾压的血肉之躯

摩羯座 / Capricorn

050

The mind, sharp but not broad, sticks at every point but does not move.

051

Your idol is shattered in the dust to prove that God's dust is greater than your idol.

思想，锐利但不够开阔

则执着有余，灵活不足

你的偶像破碎于尘埃

证明你的偶像

望上帝之尘而莫及

Man does not reveal himself in his history, he struggles up through it.

水瓶座 / Aquarius

人不坦露自己的过去

而总想从中挣脱

双鱼座 / Pisces

053

While the glass lamp rebukes the earthen for calling it cousin, the moon rises, and the glass lamp, with a bland smile, calls her, "My dear, dear sister."

054

Like the meeting of the seagulls and the waves we meet and come near. The seagulls fly off, the waves roll away and we depart.

玻璃灯责备瓦灯称呼其为表哥
此时，月亮升起
玻璃灯淡然一笑，呼唤月亮——
“我亲……亲爱的妹妹。”

就像海鸥与海浪的相遇
我们相遇相知
当海鸥飞走，海浪翻去
我们分离了

马丁·R. 巴延斯 Martin R. Baeyens 享誉世界的油画、版画艺术家和设计师，比利时根特皇家美术学院设计学院终身教授。1943 年生于比利时梅勒。在世界各地举办个人展览 128 次，参加了 1109 次国内外团体展，166 次获得国际奖项，并多次担任国际展览评委，在世界版画界享有举足轻重的地位。在比利时根特皇家美术学院设计学院任教 40 年。在伊拉斯谟国际教育交流项目中，被邀请到巴塞罗那、里斯本、克拉科夫、利默里克授课，并于近年来受邀在中国的多所大学授课。作品多以自然为主题，使用电子线路印刷技术，不断探索自然和技术的平衡。版画则以丝网技术为特点，技艺炉火纯青。身为一个完美主义者，他始终坚持亲力亲为，至今已创作并制作了 882 件作品，并在生命的过程中不断注解自己、呈现自己。

基于对世界各地丰富历史文物的欣赏与尊重，我对星座进行了全新的创作。我的作品把十二个星座与数个世纪以来丝绸之路上交易的丝织品相结合。通过我的新作，十二星座重回中国。

马丁 · R. 巴延斯

I created a totally new representation of the zodiac based on appreciation and respect of artifacts of our rich past across all continents. All the twelves elements from the zodiac were all integrated on a background of silk fabrics traded over the centuries on the silk route and are now again re-entered by me in my new Zodiac images into China.

Martin R.Baeyens

Ik ontwierp een drietal nieuwe dinerserviezen op basis van waardering en respect voor artefacten uit het rijke verleden van alle continenten.

Alle twaalf elementen uit de dinerserviezen zijn geïntegreerd op een achtergrond van zijden stoffen die door de eeuwen heen op de zijderoute werden verhandeld. Deze ontwerpen werden door mij via deze weg opnieuw ingevoerd in China.

Smetlede Belgium.
05-05-2010

Thank th

flame for it

light, but d

not forget th

lamphold

standing i

the shade wit

constancy c

patienc

055

My day is done, and I am like a boat drawn on the beach, listening to the dance-music of the tide in the evening.

白羊座 / Aries

一日终了

我如一叶扁舟疲惫地靠在海滩

聆听夜幕下的涛声舞曲

金牛座 / Taurus

056

Life is given to us,

we earn it by giving it.

057

We come nearest to the great when

we are great in humility.

生命来自天赐
我们奉献生命
方能赢得生命

谦谦君子
近乎伟人

058

The sparrow is sorry for the peacock
at the burden of its tail.

059

Never be afraid of the moments—
thus sings the voice of the
everlasting.

麻雀为孔雀惋惜

拖着尾巴多累赘

不要畏惧瞬间

——永恒之声唱道

060

The hurricane seeks the shortest road by the no-road, and suddenly ends its search in the Nowhere.

双子座 / Gemini

为寻捷径，飓风慌不择路

结果却是突然间走投无路

巨蟹座 / Cancer

061

Take my wine in my own cup, friend.
It loses its wreath of foam when poured
into that of others.

062

The Perfect decks itself in beauty
for the love of the Imperfect.

朋友，我用自己的杯子

敬你这杯酒

如果倒入别人的杯子

你就看不到酒沫的涟漪

出于对“不完美”的爱

“完美”扮靓自己

063

God says to man, “I heal you therefore I hurt, love you therefore punish.”

064

Thank the flame for its light, but do not forget the lampholder standing in the shade with constancy of patience.

上帝对人说：

我因给你治病而受伤，

我因爱你而惩罚你。

感谢火焰的光芒

但勿忘黑暗中锲而不舍的掌灯人

065

Tiny grass, your steps are small, but you possess the earth under your tread.

狮子座 / Leo

小草，你举步维艰

但你拥有脚下的大地

处女座 / Virgo

066

The infant flower opens its bud and
cries, "Dear World, please do not fade."

067

God grows weary of great kingdoms,
but never of little flowers.

蓓蕾初放的花朵吐露心声：

亲爱的世界，请勿凋零

上帝渐渐厌倦了伟大的王国

但始终青睐小小的花朵

068

Wrong cannot afford defeat but Right can.

069

“I give my whole water in joy,”sings the waterfall, “though little of it is enough for the thirsty.”

错，一败涂地

对，虽败犹荣

“我乐于献出我全部的水，”瀑布唱道，

“尽管一丁点就足以解渴。”

Where is the fountain that
throws up these flowers in a
ceaseless outbreak of ecstasy?

天秤座 / Libra

繁花争艳，怒放不止

试问花香何处来

天蝎座 / Scorpio

071

The woodcutter's axe begged
for its handle from the tree.
The tree gave it.

072

In my solitude of heart I feel the sigh of
this widowed evening veiled with mist
and rain.

伐木的斧头向树
索求一根木柄
树成全了它

此夜
孑然一身
雨雾遮蒙
我心
最隐处
听到夜的叹息

073

Chastity is a wealth that comes
from abundance of love.

074

The mist, like love, plays upon
the heart of the hills and
brings out surprises of beauty.

忠贞无价

源自磅礴的爱

雾如爱般妩媚

拨动山的心弦

生出无数美的惊叹

075

We read the world wrong and say

that it deceives us.

射手座 / Sagittarius

我们误读了世界

却说世界欺骗了我们

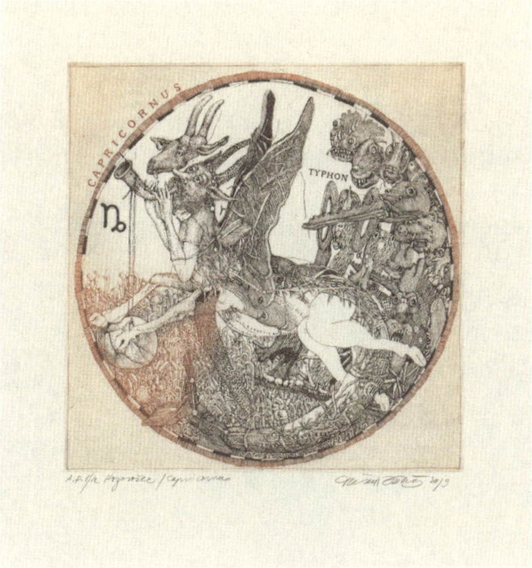

摩羯座 / Capricorn

076

The poet wind is out over the sea and the forest to seek his own voice.

077

Every child comes with the message that God is not yet discouraged of man.

诗人的气息

穿越大海和森林

他在寻找属于自己的声音

每一个孩子的降生

都传递出这样一个信息：

上帝尚未对人类失去信心

078

The grass seeks her crowd in the earth.

The tree seeks his solitude of the sky.

079

Man barricades against himself.

草在地上寻找她的同伴

树向空中寻找他的孤独

人总是作茧自缚

080

Your voice, my friend, wanders in my heart, like the muffled sound of the sea among these listening pines.

水瓶座 / Aquarius

朋友，你的声音徘徊在我的心间

宛若松林在聆听大海的低吟

双鱼座 / Pisces

081

What is this unseen flame of darkness whose sparks are the stars?

082

Let life be beautiful like summer flowers and death like autumn leaves.

黑暗中一种看不见的火焰
它的火花飞溅出满天繁星
这火焰是什么呢

让生美如夏花
让死美若秋叶

083

He who wants to do good knocks at the gate; he who loves finds the gate open.

084

In death the many becomes one; in life the one becomes many.

Religion will be one when God is dead.

门，等欲行善之人去叩响
对常行仁爱之人敞开

死时，万物合一
生时，一生万物
上帝死了，信仰归一

我的星座系列绘画作品深受远古星座故事的启发。我从希腊神话中学习良多。这是一件很有趣的工作，我相信我的作品也会很有意思。

杜桑 · 凯利

In my zodiac works, I was inspirited by ancient zodiac stories. I learned a lot about it from Greek mythology. It was very interesting work and I believe, that it will be interesting.

Dusan Kallay

杜桑·凯利　Dusan Kallay　布拉迪斯拉发美术学院插画系和版画系教授，BIB终身荣誉奖获得者，斯洛伐克国宝级艺术家。1948年出生于斯洛伐克布拉迪斯拉发。1966年至1972年就读于布拉迪斯拉发美术学院，师承文森特·何塞克与詹力布斯基。1990年起在布拉迪斯拉发艺术大学教授插画、油画、版画、邮票设计、海报与卡通等课程，是欧洲铜版之父阿尔滨·布鲁诺夫斯基的继任者。杜桑·凯利被誉为东欧魔幻艺术巨匠，他是首位、也是唯一一位同时获得国际安徒生大奖和布拉迪斯国际插画双年展（BIB）首奖殊荣的艺术家，创下了150多次国际巡回个展，46项国际大奖的辉煌纪录，拥有我们熟知的博洛尼亚国际童书插画大奖、巴塞罗那国际插画双年展特别奖、联合国儿童救援基金会年度最佳插画家、BIB终身荣誉奖在内的殊荣。杜桑·凯利迄今完成了200余本童书插画，包括《爱丽丝梦游仙境》《蟋蟀与蚂蚁》《斯洛伐克童话》和《王尔德童话》等世界经典童话故事，以及莎士比亚的《仲夏夜之梦》和《威尼斯商人》等名著，被无数国际插画名家奉为导师。

V mojej práci som sa inšpiroval
starými príbehmi zodiaku a tiež
gréckou mytológiou.
Bola to veľmi zaujímavá práca
a verím že nájde veľa potešenia
náročného výtvaru a čitateľa
pripravovanej knihy.

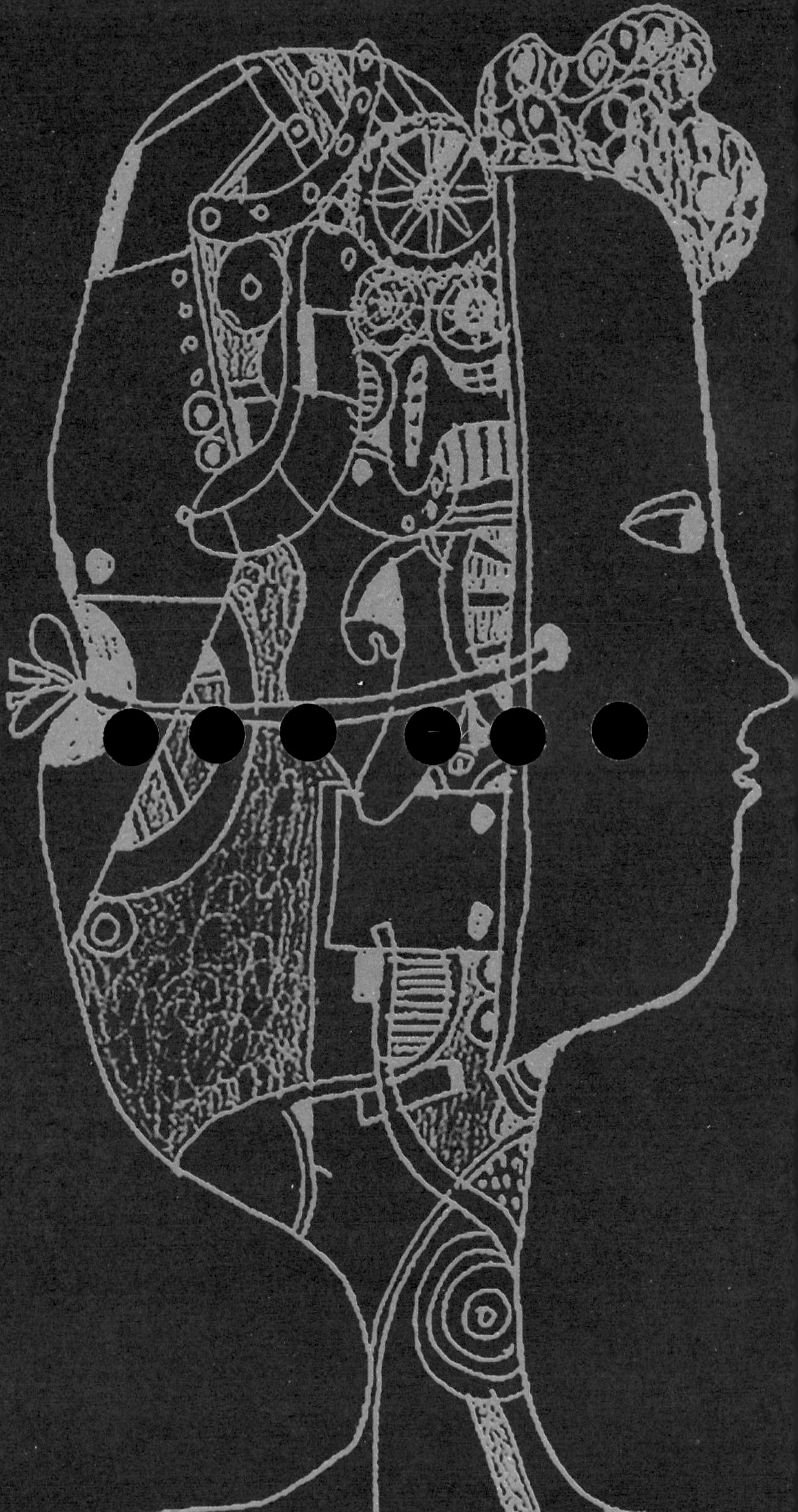

I think o
other ages tha
floated upo
the stream o
life and love an
death and ar
forgotten, and
feel the freedor
of passing awa

085

The artist is the lover of Nature, therefore he is her slave and her master.

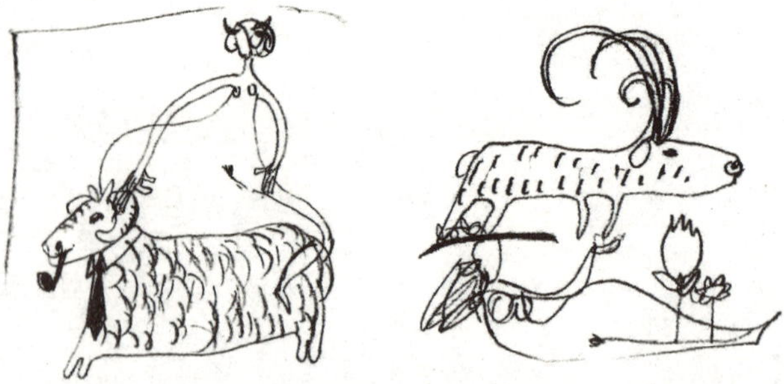

艺术家是大自然的情人
因此，他既是她的奴隶
又是她的主人

白羊座 / Aries

086

"How far are you from me, O Fruit?"

"I am hidden in your heart, O Flower."

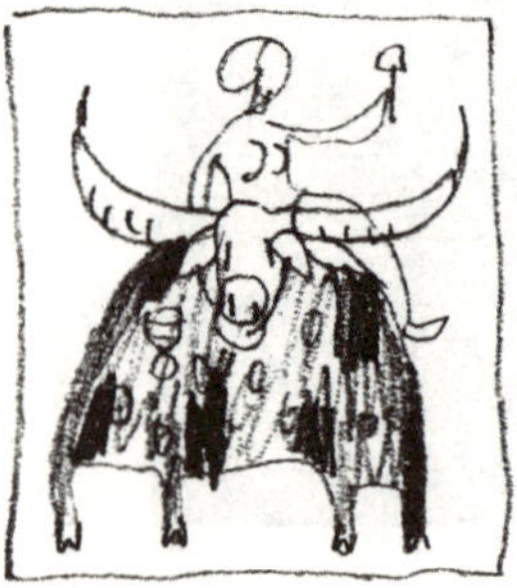

“哦，果实，你离我有多远？”

“哦，花儿，我藏在你的心里呢。”

金牛座 / Taurus

087

This longing is for the one who is felt in the dark, but not seen in the day.

088

"You are the big drop of dew under the lotus leaf, I am the smaller one on its upper side," said the dewdrop to the lake.

这份渴望只为一个人

夜相逢

日无踪

“你是荷叶下面的一颗大露珠，

我是荷叶上面的一颗小露珠。”

露珠对湖水如是说。

089

The scabbard is content to
be dull when it protects the
keenness of the sword.

090

In darkness the One appears as uniform;
in the light the One appears as manifold.

为保护剑的锋芒
鞘自甘愚钝

黑暗中，“一”求同
光明中，“一”存异

160

The great earth makes herself hospitable

with the help of the grass.

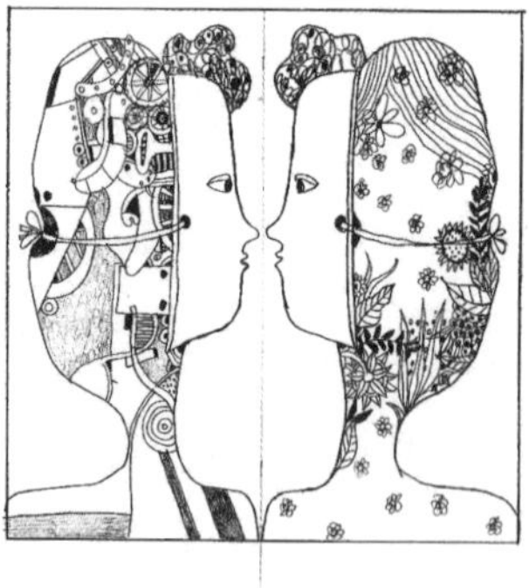

芳草助大地更加好客

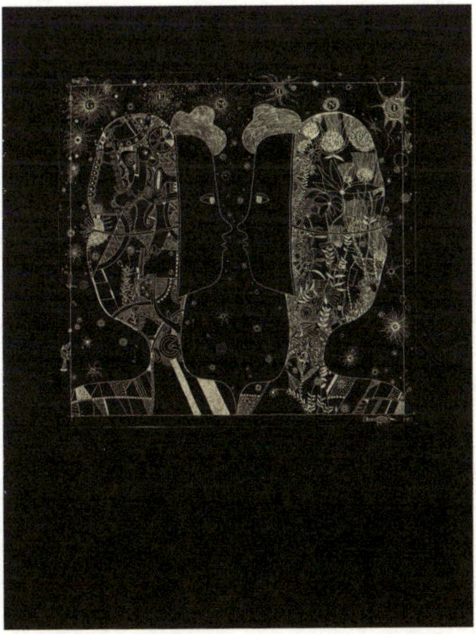

双子座 / Gemini

092

The birth and death of the leaves are
the rapid whirls of the eddy whose
wider circles move slowly among stars.

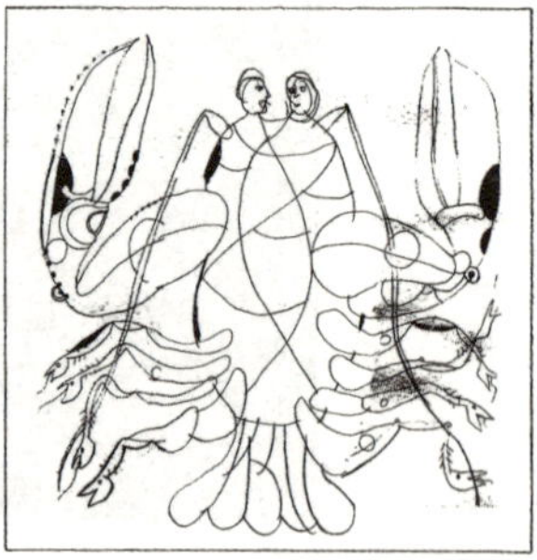

树叶的生死轮回犹如快速旋转的漩涡
而漩涡的外圈是天体缓慢运行的轨道

巨蟹座 / Cancer

093

Power said to the world, “You are mine.”

The world kept it prisoner on her throne.

Love said to the world, “I am thine.”

The world gave it the freedom of her

house.

094

The mist is like the earth’s desire.

It hides the sun for whom she cries.

权力对世界说：
“你是属于我的。”
世界便把权力囚禁于她的王位
爱情对世界说：
“我是属于你的。”
世界便将她自由的殿堂赠予爱情

雾就像是大地的渴望
她呼叫太阳
却遮蔽了太阳

095

Be still, my heart, these great trees
are prayers.

请安静

我的心啊

大树们正在祈祷

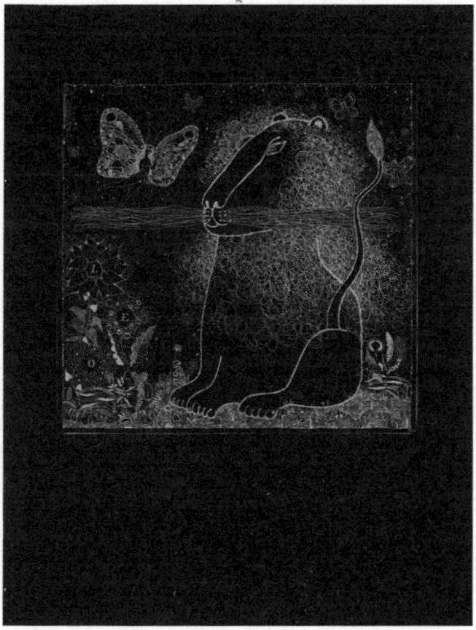

狮子座 / Leo

096

The noise of the moment scoffs at

the music of the Eternal.

瞬间的喧嚣

嘲笑永恒的音乐

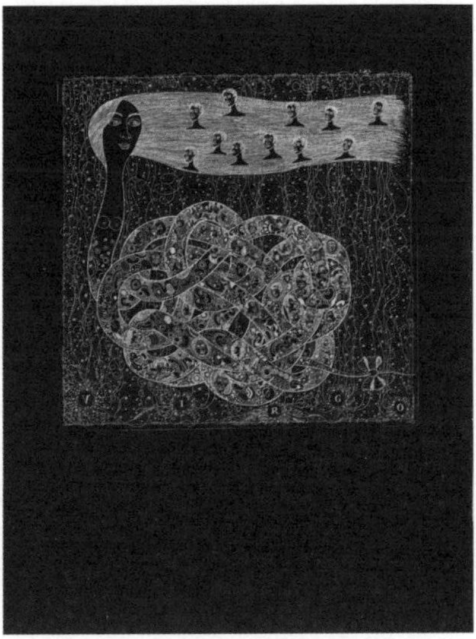

处女座 / Virgo

097

I think of other ages that floated upon the stream of life and love and death and are forgotten, and I feel the freedom of passing away.

098

The sadness of my soul is her bride's veil. It waits to be lifted in the night.

想想那些逝去的年代
曾经漂浮在生与死爱与恨的溪流之上
如今皆被遗忘
于是，我对死亡越发超然度外了

我灵魂的悲伤犹如新娘的面纱
要等到夜晚方能摘下

099

Death's stamp gives value to the coin of life; making it possible to buy with life what is truly precious.

死亡的背书给生命之币注入价值

以此购得人生真正的瑰宝

天秤座 / Libra

100

The cloud stood humbly in a corner of the sky.
The morning crowned it with splendour.

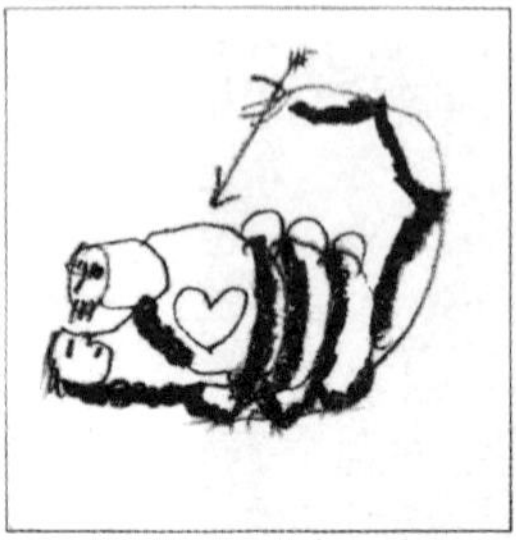

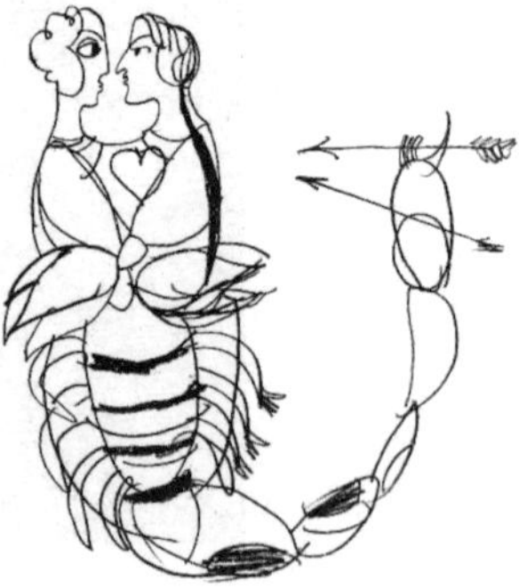

云谦卑地立于天之一隅

黎明为它辉煌加冕

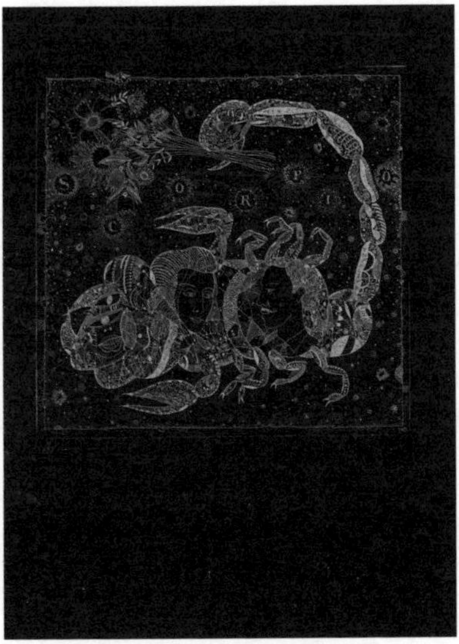

天蝎座 / Scorpio

101

The dust receives insult and in return offers her flowers.

102

Do not linger to gather flowers to keep them, but walk on, for flowers will keep themselves blooming all your way.

泥土受到侮辱

却回馈她鲜花

别为了采花而逗留

继续前行

鲜花将为你全程盛开

103

Roots are the branches down in the earth.

Branches are roots in the air.

根是深入地下的枝
枝是伸向空中的根

射手座 / Sagittarius

104

The music of the far-away summer flutters around the Autumn seeking its former nest.

远去的夏日

余音袅袅

不绝于秋

似乎要找回昔日的音盒

摩羯座 / Capricorn

105

Do not insult your friend by lending him merits from your own pocket.

106

The touch of the nameless days
clings to my heart like mosses
round the old tree.

试图向别人输出自己的美德
这是对朋友的一种侮辱

那些难以名状的日子
就像缠绕老树的苔藓
在我的心中挥之不去

107

The echo mocks her origin to prove

she is the original.

回音嘲笑她的原声

以证明她才是原声

水瓶座 / Aquarius

108

God is ashamed when the prosperous boasts of His special favour.

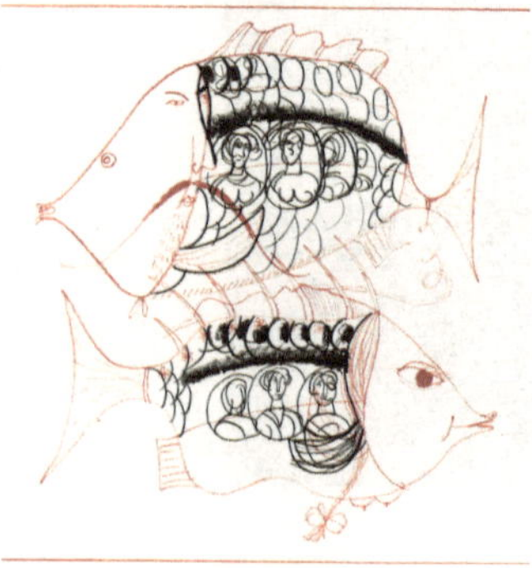

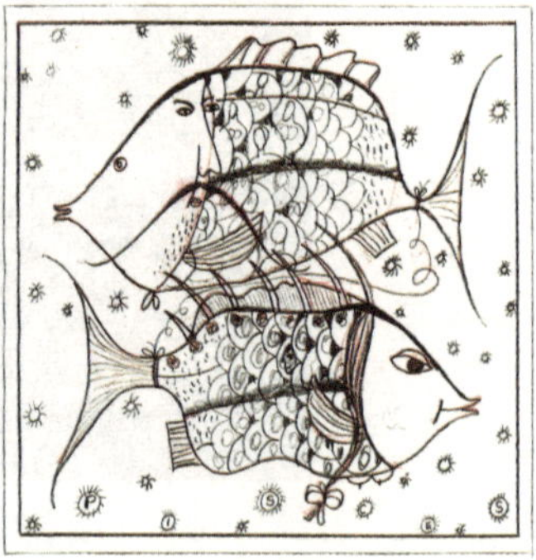

那些功成名就者自诩受神特别恩典时

上帝害羞了

双鱼座 / Pisces

Знаки Зодиака с давних пор наблюдают и вмешиваются в нашу жизнь. Все они, особенно Лев, внимательно следят за тем, как живёт и совершенствуется человек. Как личности люди сформировались не сразу, это рассказал нам Чарльз Дарвин. Сначала жили люди на деревьях и их было совсем мало. Знакам Зодиака стало скучно, между собой они давно всё обсудили. Захотелось им пообщаться с людьми, но люди прятались в густой листве и побаивались клешней Рака. Остальных Знаков Зодиака они не боялись. Однажды Лев был в хорошем настроении и подарил людям ножницы. Что такое ножницы, люди не знали. Лев продемонстрировал людям, для чего они нужны, не просто же, чтобы на дереве зря висеть. Взял и постриг львицу. И тут же отдал ножницы любопытному человеческому индивиду. А львица до сих пор ходит постриженная. Да и люди все постриглись. Потом Лев прочёл лекцию о любви к детям. И люди сразу поняли, что дети – это хорошо. Спусти [redacted] с [redacted] вье [redacted] дь на [redacted] ев [redacted] гро [redacted] вать детей очень неудобно, и всё сразу наладилось. Детей прибавилось, людей стало больше. Так на планете появилась человеческая цивилизация уважающая Знаки Зодиака. Теперь Знакам было с кем поговорить. Тем более, что общаться стало интереснее. Люди под мудрым руководством Знаков стали умнее, начитаннее, вежливее и талантливее. А в Китае до сих пор растёт одно очень старое дерево. И на нём висят те самые ножницы.

Лаздин

尤里·诺兹德林 Yuriy Nozdrin

国际艺术家联合会＆俄罗斯艺术家联盟成员，俄罗斯版画藏书票爱好者协会成员，民间艺术研究会成员。1949 年出生于立陶宛克莱佩达。1966 年至 1972 年就读于莫斯科 1905 革命纪念艺术学校。1974 年至 1980 年就读于俄罗斯工艺美术大学。尤里·诺兹德林是国际版画藏书票界公认的大师级艺术家，并屡获盛誉，1989 年至今获得包括 4 项国际金奖在内的 17 项国际比赛的奖项，并举办过 12 次个展，参加过 150 次联展。设计了大约 200 本书籍的插图，创作了 500 多幅铜版画和 270 余幅版画藏书票，100 余件手工编写装订的限量版手稿册。

十二星座长期以来一直在注视和介入我们的生活。所有这些星座，尤其狮子座，密切观察着一个人是如何生活并改善他自己的。

尤里·诺兹德林

The zodiac signs have long been watching and interfering in our lives. All of them, especially Leo, closely monitor how a person lives and improves himself.

Yuriy Nozdrin

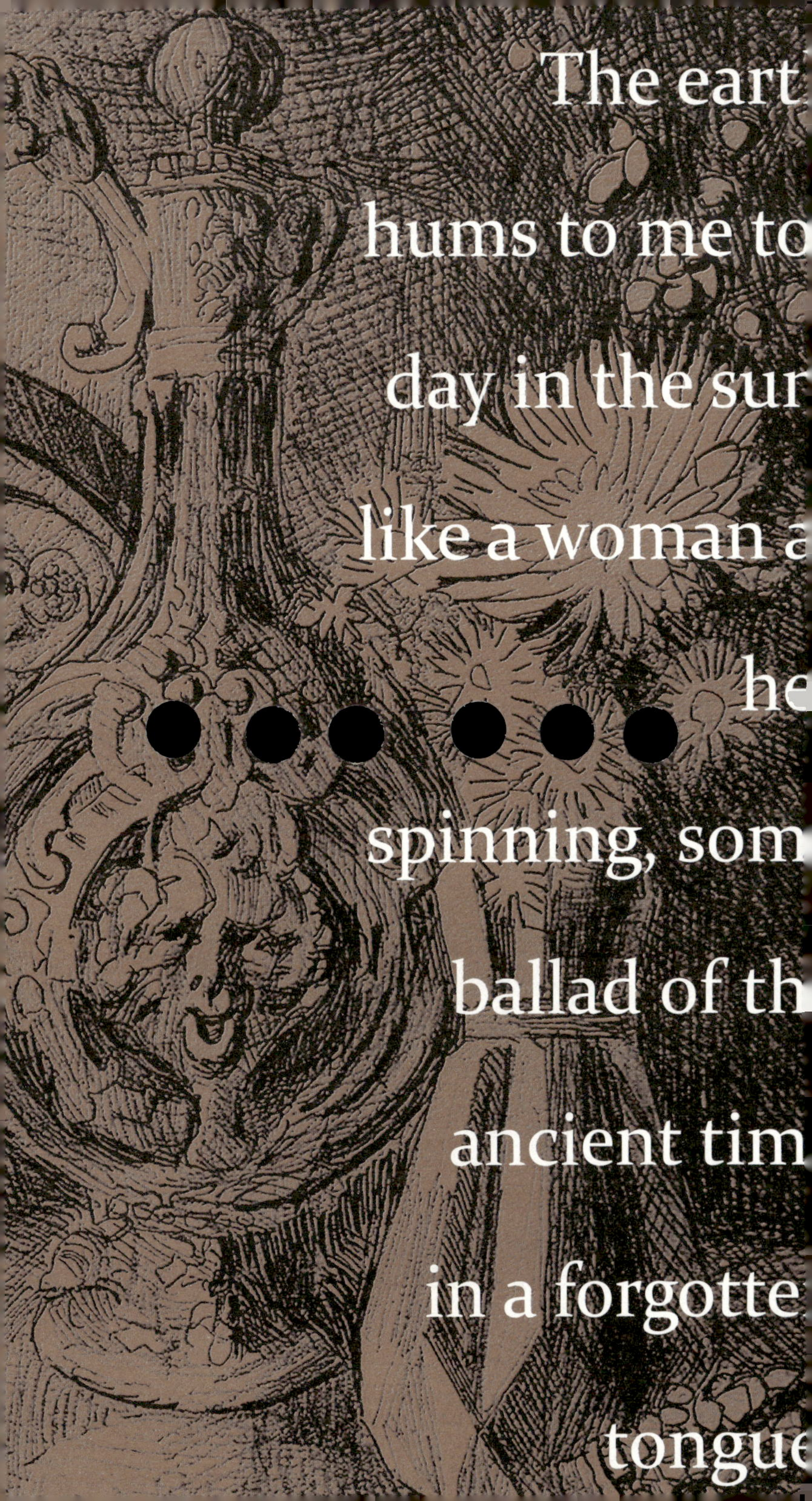

The eart

hums to me to

day in the sur

like a woman a

he

spinning, som

ballad of th

ancient tim

in a forgotte

tongue

109

I cast my own shadow upon my path, because I have a lamp that has not been lighted.

白羊座 / Aries

我把自己的影子投在我的路上

因为我有一盏灯尚未点亮

金牛座 / Taurus

110

Man goes into the noisy crowd to
drown his own clamour of silence.

111

That which ends in exhaustion is death,
but the perfect ending is in the endless.

人走进喧嚣的人群

是为了平复内心压抑的呼号

气数耗尽，则寿终正寝

善始善终，则死而不亡

112

The sun has his simple robe of light. The clouds are decked with gorgeousness.

113

The hills are like shouts of children who raise their arms, trying to catch stars.

太阳身着简约的光袍
云朵穿着绚丽的霓裳

山峦犹如欢呼的孩子
举起手臂去采摘星斗

The road is lonely in its crowd

for it is not loved.

双子座 / Gemini

无人疼爱

道路在拥堵中倍感孤独

巨蟹座 / Cancer

115

The power that boasts of its mischiefs is laughed at by the yellow leaves that fall, and clouds that pass by.

116

The earth hums to me to-day in the sun, like a woman at her spinning, some ballad of the ancient time in a forgotten tongue.

权力

不仅为非作歹

还以此自夸

连飘零的黄叶和

过眼的云烟都嘲笑它

今天

大地在阳光下

向我哼唱

仿佛一位纺线女

用被遗忘的曲调

唱着远古的民谣

117

The grass-blade is worthy of the great world where it grows.

118

Dream is a wife who must talk.
Sleep is a husband who silently suffers.

小草无愧于
它所生长的伟大世界

睡梦是一个健谈的妻子
睡眠是一个缄默的丈夫

119

The night kisses the fading day whispering to his ear, "I am death, your mother. I am to give you fresh birth."

狮子座 / Leo

夜亲吻着渐逝的白昼

在他的耳边低语：

我是死亡——你的母亲

我会给你新生

处女座 / Virgo

120

I feel, thy beauty, dark night, like that of the loved woman when she has put out the lamp.

121

I carry in my world that flourishes the worlds that have failed.

黑夜，我感受到你的美妙
恰如熄灯时刻的可爱女人

我把破败的前世
带入繁华的今生

122

Dear friend, I feel the silence of your great thoughts of many a deepening eventide on this beach when I listen to these waves.

123

The bird thinks it is an act of kindness to give the fish a lift in the air.

亲爱的朋友
多少个深沉的黄昏
在这个岸边听涛声响起
我领悟到你伟大思想的静寂

鸟儿以为
它把鱼儿叼出水面是一个善举

124

"In the moon thou sendest thy love letters to me," said the night to the sun.
"I leave my answers in tears upon the grass."

天秤座 / Libra

"你从月亮上给我寄送情书，"
夜对太阳说，
"我用泪水把回复留在芳草上。"

天蝎座 / Scorpio

125

The Great is a born child; when he dies he gives his great childhood to the world.

126

Not hammerstrokes, but dance of the water sings the pebbles into perfection.

伟人天生就是孩童
离世时，他把伟大的童真
留给世界

不靠人工捶打
流水的欢歌和舞蹈
造就了鹅卵石的完美

127

Bees sip honey from flowers and hum their thanks when they leave.
The gaudy butterfly is sure that the flowers owe thanks to him.

128

To be outspoken is easy when you do not wait to speak the complete truth.

蜜蜂在花丛中啜蜜
离开时总不忘嗡嗡道谢

而恶俗的蝴蝶总觉得
是鲜花欠了他的人情

直言不讳并不难
你只需说出部分真相

129

Asks the Possible to the Impossible,

"Where is your dwelling place?"

"In the dreams of the impotent,"

comes the answer.

射手座 / Sagittarius

"可能"问"不可能"：

"你住在何处？"

"我住在无能者的梦里。"

"不可能"答道。

摩羯座 / Capricorn

130

If you shut your door to all errors truth will be shut out.

131

I hear some rustle of things behind my sadness of heart,—I cannot see them.

如果你把所有的错误都拒之门外

真理也难幸免

我听到内心悲伤背后的响动

——但我看不见它

132

Leisure in its activity is work.

The stillness of the sea stirs in waves.

133

The leaf becomes flower when it loves.

The flower becomes fruit when it worships.

闲暇转为行动即可有所作为

犹如大海的平静孕育着波澜

恋爱令枝叶开花

崇拜令花儿结果

The roots below the earth claim no rewards for making the branches fruitful.

水瓶座 / Aquarius

枝叶繁茂，果实累累

但地下的根从不邀功求赏

双鱼座 / Pisces

135

This rainy evening the wind is restless.
I look at the swaying branches and ponder
over the greatness of all things.

136

Storm of midnight, like a giant child
awakened in the untimely dark,has
begun to play and shout.

风雨交加之夜
我凝望摇曳的枝丫
感悟万物之灵

午夜的风暴
如一个在黑暗中
提前醒来的巨婴
开始玩耍、叫嚷

137

Thou raisest thy waves vainly to follow thy lover. O sea, thou lonely bride of the storm.

138

"I am ashamed of my emptiness," said the Word to the Work.

"I know how poor I am when I see you," said the Work to the Word.

哦，大海
你是暴风雨的
孤独的新娘
你徒劳地掀起波浪
去追随你的爱人

“我羞于我的空洞。”
词语对作品说。
“看到你，我就知道我有多贫乏了。”
作品对词语说。

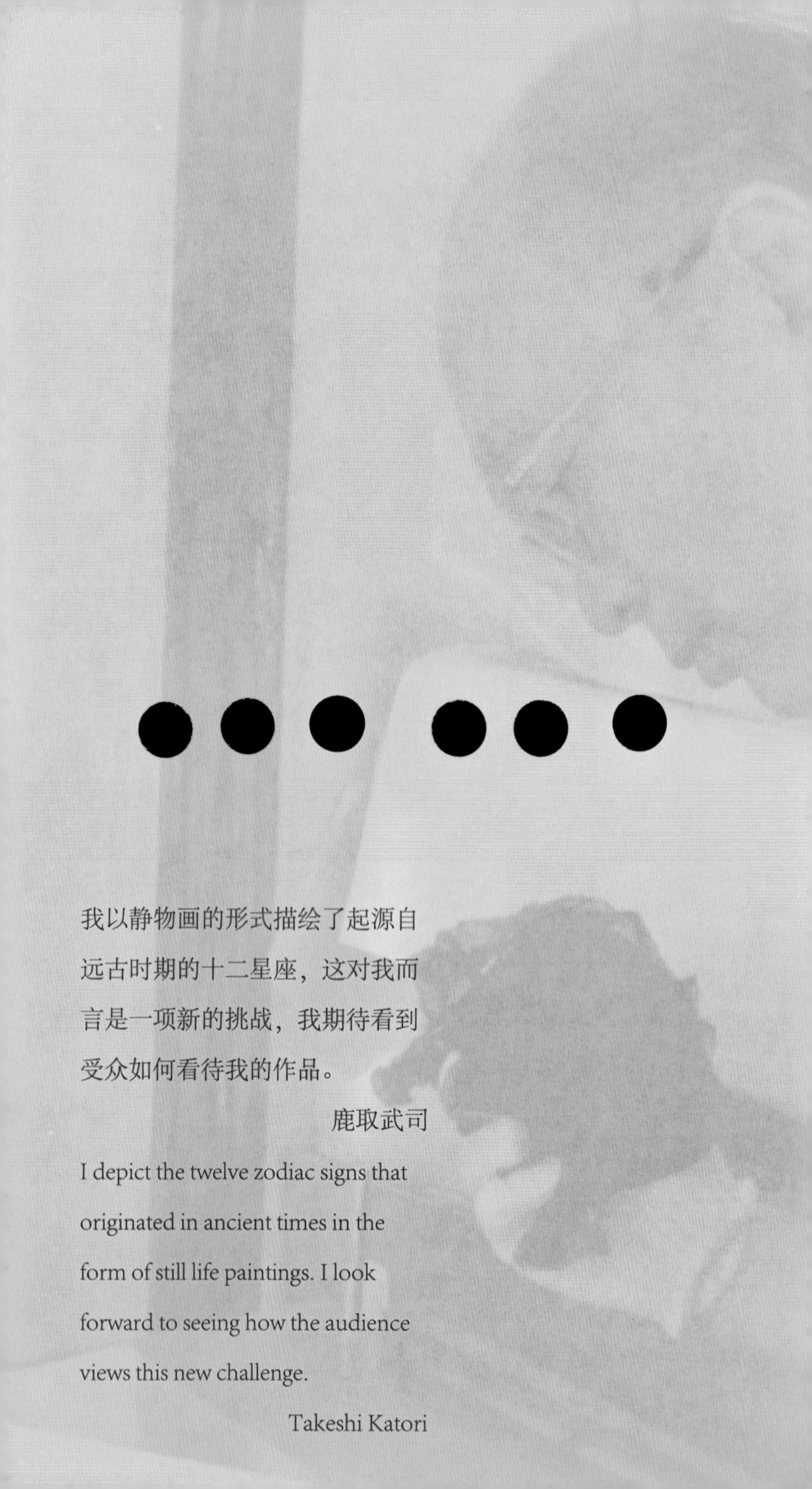

我以静物画的形式描绘了起源自远古时期的十二星座，这对我而言是一项新的挑战，我期待看到受众如何看待我的作品。

鹿取武司

I depict the twelve zodiac signs that originated in ancient times in the form of still life paintings. I look forward to seeing how the audience views this new challenge.

Takeshi Katori

鹿取武司 Takeshi Katori 大学版画学会会员，日本美术家联盟会员，日本藏书票协会会员，元文化女子大学教授、日本“美柔汀”版画代表人物之一。1949年出生于日本东京。1978年研究生毕业于东京学艺大学大学院。1981年以来，举办个人画展49次，参加日本、法国、美国、南斯拉夫、澳大利亚、波兰、韩国、德国、意大利、西班牙、比利时、印度、保加利亚、俄罗斯、加拿大、中国等群展数十次。自1985年第四届美国洛克福特国际版画双年展获大会最高奖以来，多次在国际展览上获奖。“美柔汀”是铜版画的一种特有制版方法，以日本最为繁盛。其效果细腻、视觉柔和，流传已久，独具魅力，这种方法不使用酸腐蚀和雕刀镌刻，而是依靠一种特制的摇凿，做出密密的毛点，造成一片黑色，然后再通过刮刀和压力把这些毛点不同程度地刮平压平，显出不同的明暗层次而制作出图像来。几个世纪以来一直被用来复制油画和肖像，到现在又被版画家用来制作一些特殊效果的版画。

私は古い起源を持つ12星座物語を静物画として表現した。
この新たな挑戦がどう見られるのか楽しみである。

鹿取武司

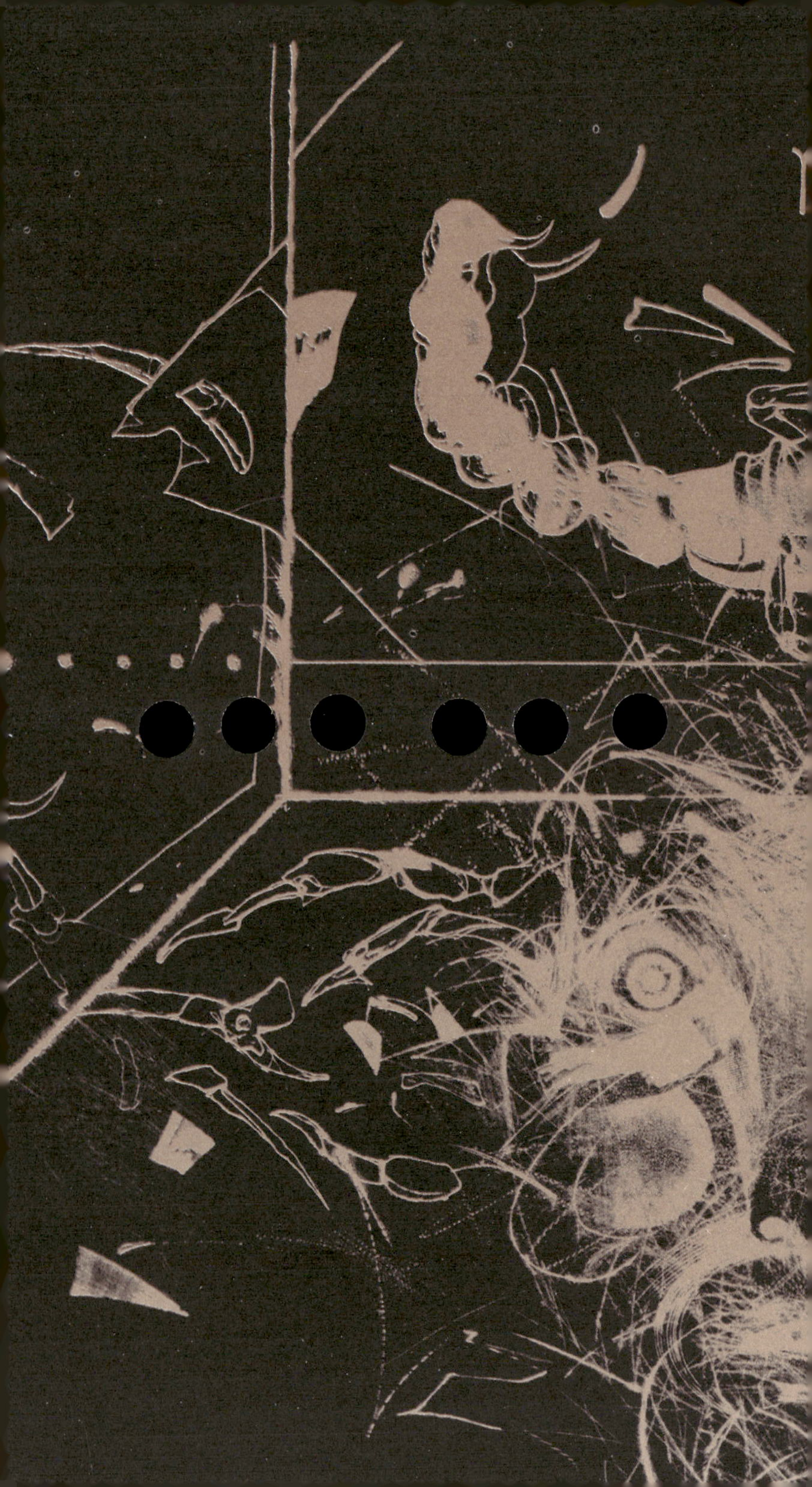

When I travelle

to here and t

there, I was tire

of thee, O Roa

but now whe

thou leadest m

to everywhere

am wedded t

thee in lov

Time is the wealth of change, but the clock in its parody makes it mere change and no wealth.

白羊座 / Aries

时间在变化中创造价值

而时钟只是拙劣地模仿

虽然变化但不创造任何价值

金牛座 / Taurus

140

Truth in her dress finds facts too tight.

In fiction she moves with ease.

141

When I travelled to here and to there, I was tired of thee, O Road, but now when thou leadest me to everywhere I am wedded to thee in love.

真理

穿上事实的外衣

倍感拘束

换上虚构的外衣

则宽松自在

哦，道路

过去我四处奔波的时候

曾对你产生过厌倦

可现在

当你引领我走向四方的时候

我与你相爱相依

142

Let me think that there is one among
those stars that guides my life
through the dark unknown.

143

Woman, with the grace of your fingers
you touched my things and order came
out like music.

我相信，满天繁星中必有一颗

指引我的人生穿越未知的黑暗

女人，你用优雅的手指

触摸我的一切，这一切

便如音乐般井然有序了

144

One sad voice has its nest among the ruins of the years.
It sings to me in the night,—"I loved you."

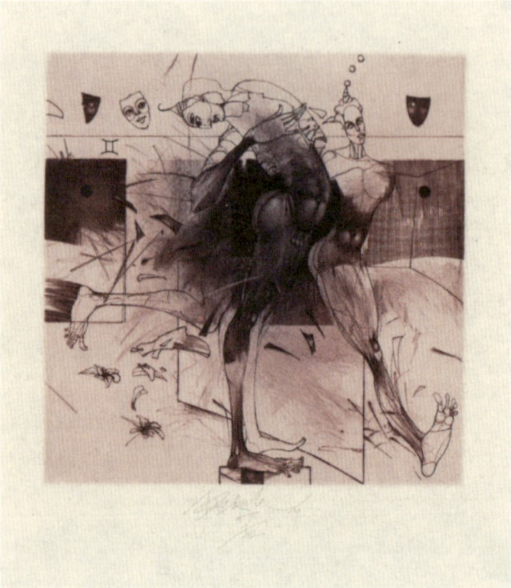

双子座 / Gemini

一个悲伤的声音

在岁月的废墟上筑巢

深夜对我歌唱——

我爱过你

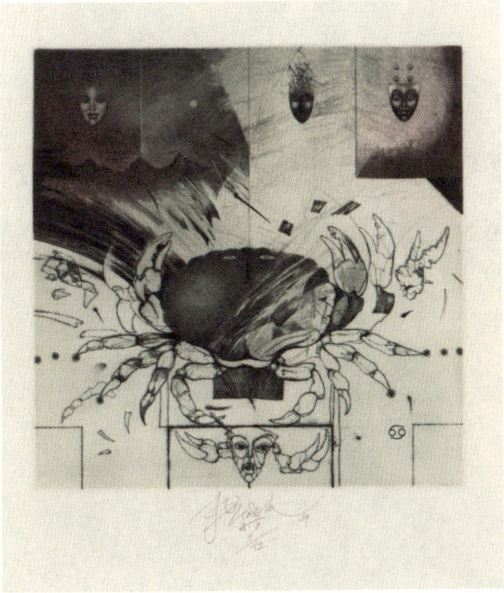

巨蟹座 / Cancer

145

The flaming fire warns me off by its own glow.
Save me from the dying embers hidden under ashes.

146

I have my stars in the sky, but oh for my little lamp unlit in my house.

熊熊的烈火用灼热警告我离开
将我从死灰余烬中解救出来吧

我拥有满天繁星
可家里那盏小灯却未点亮

147

The dust of the dead words clings to thee.

Wash thy soul with silence.

148

Gaps are left in life through which

comes the sad music of death.

故纸堆的灰尘挥之不去
你用沉默来洗涤灵魂吧

生命中总有一些沟沟坎坎
从那里传出忧伤的死亡之曲

149

The world has opened its heart of light in the morning. Come out, my heart, with thy love to meet it.

狮子座 / Leo

清晨，世界敞开它光明的心扉

出来，我的心，携爱与之相会

处女座 / Virgo

150

My thoughts shimmer with these shimmering leaves and my heart sings with the touch of this sunlight; my life is glad to be floating with all things into the blue of space, into the dark of time.

151

God's great power is in the gentle breeze, not in the storm.

我的思想随树叶的闪烁而闪烁
我的心灵随阳光的抚摸而歌唱
我的生命愿随世间万物
悦然飘入蔚蓝的太空和
幽暗的时间

上帝的伟力体现在和风里
而非风暴中

152

This is a dream in which things are all loose and they oppress.
I shall find them gathered in thee when I awake and shall be free.

153

"Who is there to take up my duties?" asked the setting sun.
"I shall do what I can, my Master," said the earthen lamp.

梦中，万物既散漫又压抑
当我醒来并将获得自由时
我会发现你集二者于一身

“谁能接替我的职责？”落日问。

“主人啊，我会尽力而为的。”泥灯答道。

154

By plucking her petals you do not gather the beauty of the flower.

天秤座 / Libra

摘下花瓣

你并不能得到花的美丽

天蝎座 / Scorpio

155

Silence will carry your voice like the nest that holds the sleeping birds.

156

The Great walks with the Small
without fear.
The Middling keeps aloof.

沉默承载着你的声音

犹如鸟巢怀抱着熟睡的鸟儿

伟大从不介意与弱小同行

而中庸却避之莫及

157

The night opens the flowers in secret and allows the day to get thanks.

射手座 / Sagittarius

夜悄悄地让花儿盛开

却甘愿让白昼去接受感激

摩羯座 / Capricorn

158

Power takes as ingratitude the writhings of its victims.

159

When we rejoice in our fulness, then we can part with our fruits with joy.

强权把受害者的苦难

当作忘恩负义

当我们心满意足时

方能欣然放弃自己的果实

160

The raindrops kissed the earth and whispered,—"We are thy homesick children, mother, come back to thee from the heaven."

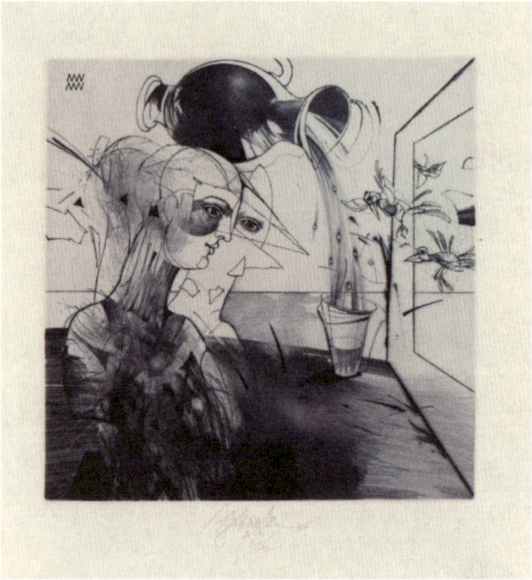

水瓶座 / Aquarius

雨滴亲吻大地并低语：

妈妈，

我们是您的孩子，

我们想家，

从天堂回来了。

双鱼座 / Pisces

161

The cobweb pretends to catch dew-drops and catches flies.

162

Love! When you come with the burning lamp of pain in your hand, I can see your face and know you as bliss.

蜘蛛网假装去捕捉露珠

然后，捕获了苍蝇

爱！当你手持炽热的痛苦之灯走来

我可以看见你的面容

知道你就是幸福的化身

163

"The learned say that your lights
will one day be no more." said
the firefly to the stars.
The stars made no answer.

164

In the dusk of the evening the bird of some early dawn comes to the nest of my silence.

"学者说有朝一日你们的光芒将会黯淡。"

萤火虫对星星说。

星星未予回答。

黄昏时分

一只黎明的鸟儿

飞进我静谧的巢

伊日·布拉兹达 Jiri Brazda 捷克视觉艺术家联盟成员，捷克版画艺术家协会成员。1952 年出生于捷克特普利采。1967 年至 1971 年就读于布拉格应用艺术学校。1973 年至 1979 年就读于布拉格应用艺术学院斯克莱纳和米库拉教授工作室，专攻版画、手绘和油画。自 1986 年以来，已举办过超过 100 次个展。在过去的三十多年里，在捷克、澳大利亚、比利时、丹麦、法国、荷兰、意大利、德国、奥地利、波兰、英国、日本、中国、美国等国家参加过 140 多次联展和主题展。自 1982 年以来，在捷克和国际上获得过 32 次奖项，特别是在版画和藏书票领域。其作品被国际上多家美术馆、艺术机构或私人藏家展示并收藏。

处理十二星座画作是一项困难艰巨的任务，同时也是一个巨大的挑战。我不是第一个或最后一个用图画来创作这一覆盖一年四季有趣轮回的人。也许我已经圆满完成了这项任务，也许我的画作会令藏家和观众满意，也许这能让我一睹占星学的世界，也许更多人能从中学到些东西。那么我如何看待占星学呢？星星永远都不说谎吗？还是我错了？

伊日 · 布拉兹达

It was a difficult and arduous task to process the twelve signs of the horoscope.But at the same time a big challenge.I was not the first or the last to graphically create this interesting cycle coverting the whole season.Perhaps I have fulfilled the task,perhaps it will please the client and the spectators,perhaps it will allow me to look into the world of astrology and it will become a lesson for many.And my opinion on the horoscope?Do the stars never lie or am I wrong?

Jiri Brazda

That whic

oppresses me, i

it my soul tryin

to come out i

the open, c

the soul of th

world knockin

at my heart fc

its entrance

Thoughts pass in my mind like flocks
of ducks in the sky.
I hear the voice of their wings.

思想在我的心中掠过

犹如野鸭在空中飞翔

我听到它们的振翅之声

白羊座 / Aries

166

The canal loves to think that rivers exist solely to supply it with water.

167

The world has kissed my soul with its pain, asking for its return in songs.

沟渠乐于认为

河流的存在只是为了给它供水

世界用痛苦亲吻我的灵魂

索取歌声作为回报

168

That which oppresses me, is
it my soul trying to come out
in the open, or the soul of the
world knocking at my heart for
its entrance?

金牛座 / Taurus

压迫我的

究竟是我的灵魂

——它欲从我的身体逃出

还是世界的灵魂

——它叩响我的心扉

试图闯入我的内心

双子座 / Gemini

169

Thought feeds itself with its own words and grows.

170

I have dipped the vessel of my heart into this silent hour; it has filled with love.

思想从自己的话语中
获得滋养，成长

我把心灵的容器
沉浸于这片沉默的时光
它便充满了爱

171

Either you have work or you have not.
When you have to say, "Let us do
something," then begins mischief.

有为还是无为

当你不得不说“我们干点什么”的时候

祸根埋下

巨蟹座 / Cancer

172

The sunflower blushed to own the nameless flower as her kin.

The sun rose and smiled on it, saying, "Are you well, my darling?"

173

"Who drives me forward like fate?"

"The Myself striding on my back."

向日葵羞于认无名花为亲
太阳升起，微笑着对无名花说：
你好吗，我亲爱的？

“是谁如命运一般催我奋进？ ”
“是‘自我’助推前行。”

174

The clouds fill the watercups of the river, hiding themselves in the distant hills.

云，注满江河

自己躲进远山

狮子座 / Leo

175

I spill water from my water jar as I walk on my way. Very little remains for my home.

我提着水罐，一路走一路洒

到家时，水所剩无几了

处女座 / Virgo

176

The water in a vessel is sparkling; the water in the sea is dark.

The small truth has words that are clear; the great truth has great silence.

器皿里的水耀眼

大海里的水黯淡

小道理意会言传

大道理不可言说

天秤座 / Libra

177

Your smile was the flowers of your own fields, your talk was the rustle of your own mountain pines, but your heart was the woman that we all know.

178

It is the little things that I leave behind for my loved ones,—great things are for everyone.

你的微笑是你田野里的鲜花
你的话语是你山林里的松涛
但你的心啊，是那位尽人皆知的女人

我把小玩意
留给我爱的人们
而伟大的物品
则留给所有人

179

Woman, thou hast encircled the world's heart with the depth of thy tears as the sea has the earth.

女人

你用深邃的泪水

拥抱世界之心

恰如大海

环抱着陆地

天蝎座 / Scorpio

180

The sunshine greets me with a smile.
The rain, his sad sister, talks to my heart.

181

My flower of the day dropped its petals forgotten.
In the evening it ripens into a golden fruit of memory.

阳光微笑着

向我问候

他忧伤的妹妹

——雨，与我的心

促膝

我的花

白天

花瓣飘零

被人遗忘

夜晚

长成熟透的金色果实

贮满记忆

182

I am like the road in the night listening to the footfalls of its memories in silence.

射手座 / Sagittarius

我就像那夜晚的道路

静静聆听记忆的足音

摩羯座 / Capricorn

183

The evening sky to me is like a window,

and a lighted lamp, and a waiting behind it.

184

He who is too busy doing good

finds no time to be good.

夜空

对于我

是一扇窗

一盏点亮的灯

以及藏在后面的

等待

他终日忙于行善

却没有时间成为善人

185

I am the autumn cloud, empty of rain, see my fulness in the field of ripened rice.

我是秋日的云朵

空虚无雨

令我充实的是

熟透了的稻田

水瓶座 / Aquarius

186

They hated and killed and men praised them.

But God in shame hastens to hide its memory under the green grass.

187

Toes are the fingers that have forsaken their past.

仇恨者、杀戮者
获得人们的赞扬
上帝羞愧难当
急忙把记忆埋藏于
绿草之下

手指背叛了自己的过去
就变成了脚趾

188

Darkness travels towards light, but blindness towards death.

黑暗走向光明

盲目走向死亡

双鱼座 / Pisces

埃米利奥·卡拉斯科·古塔雷斯 Emilio Carrasco Gutierrez　造型艺术家、策展人、萨卡特卡斯自治大学的教授、研究员。1957年出生于墨西哥。师从艺术大师 Gilberto Aceves Navarro。从1978年到1982年，先后进入西班牙的马德里私立美术学院、圣费尔南多美术学院和马德里康普顿斯大学（始建于1293年，世界古老大学之一，西班牙最顶尖公立大学）深造，曾获 Matricula de Honor 奖，西班牙文化部颁发的 Premio de adquisicion 奖，墨西哥国家造型艺术奖，Pedro Coronel 奖，意大利理想达芬奇博物馆奖和第三届国际木刻艺术大赛提名奖等，并录入萨卡特卡斯国家文化和艺术基金 Creadores con trayectoria 名录。作品在众多的大赛中入选，并被墨西哥、中美洲和欧洲的许多博物馆和画廊收藏。此外，在萨卡特卡斯自治大学发起一场极有影响力的学术活动并组建了艺术家团队，从1982年即开始在世界各地的国际视觉诗歌节上巡回展出他们的作品，这也极大地丰富了他的创作历程。现如今，已从萨卡特卡斯大学退休的他，负责弗朗西斯·戈伊蒂亚科博物馆的视觉艺术工作室，担任许多画廊的策展人，并依然从事着绘画教育工作。

艺术能够修饰万物，也能保护最伟大的创作潜能。因为艺术的创作从无到有，繁衍生命，从生命中建立秩序，由万物中创造新事物。

埃米利奥·卡拉斯科·古塔雷斯

Art has the likelihood of modifying everything and safeguarding the greatest potentials of creation, then art builds from nothing, breeds being and from being draws order, making from everything something new.

Emilio Carrasco Gutierrez

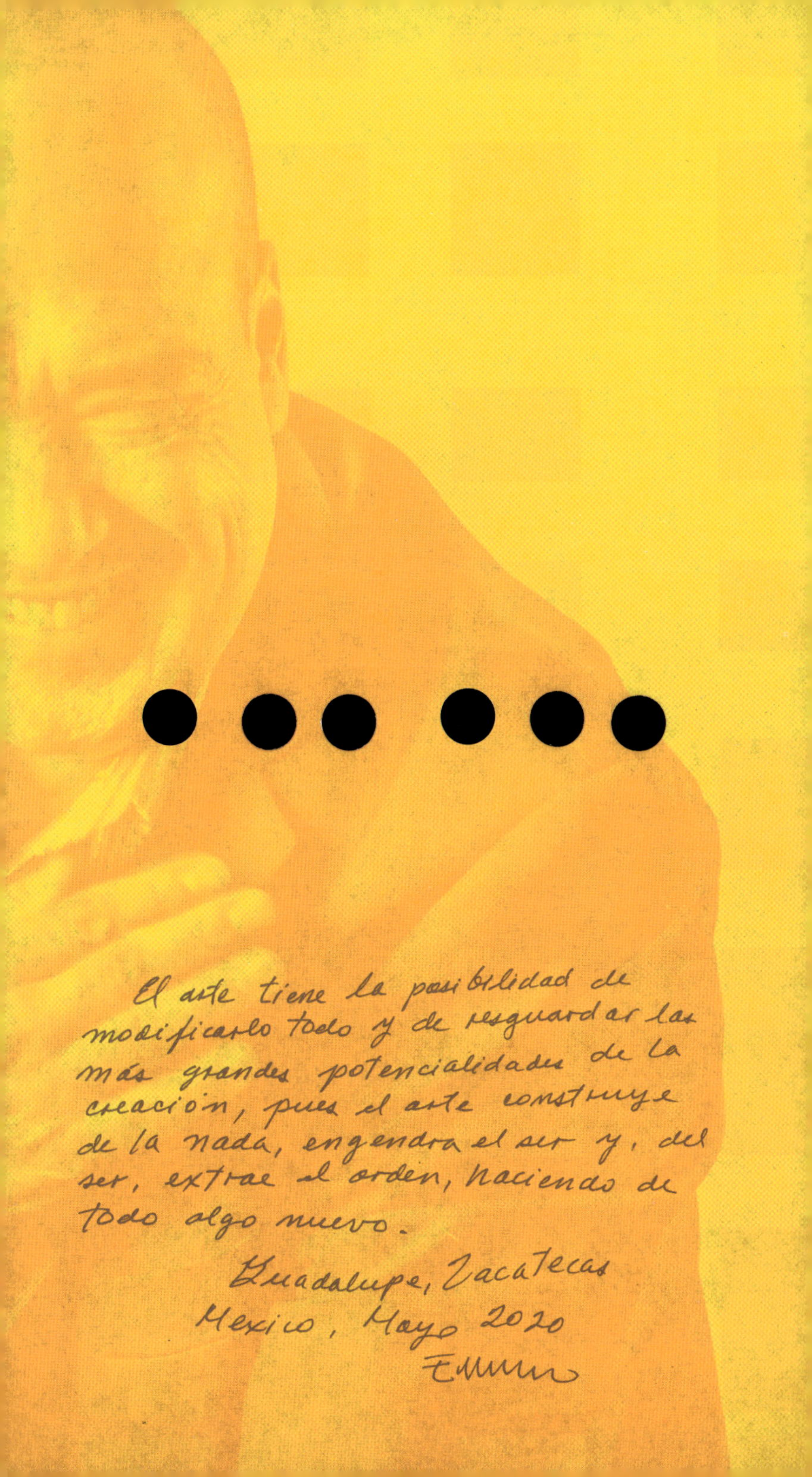

El arte tiene la posibilidad de modificarlo todo y de resguardar las más grandes potencialidades de la creación, pues el arte construye de la nada, engendra el ser y, del ser, extrae el orden, haciendo de todo algo nuevo.

Guadalupe, Zacatecas
Mexico, Mayo 2020

“My hea
is like th
golde
casket
th
kiss
said th
suns
cloud
the su

189

The pet dog suspects the universe
for scheming to take its place.

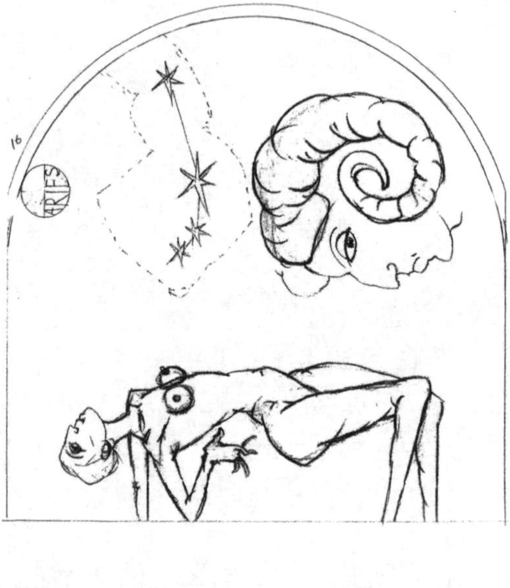

宠物狗怀疑宇宙

阴谋篡夺其地位

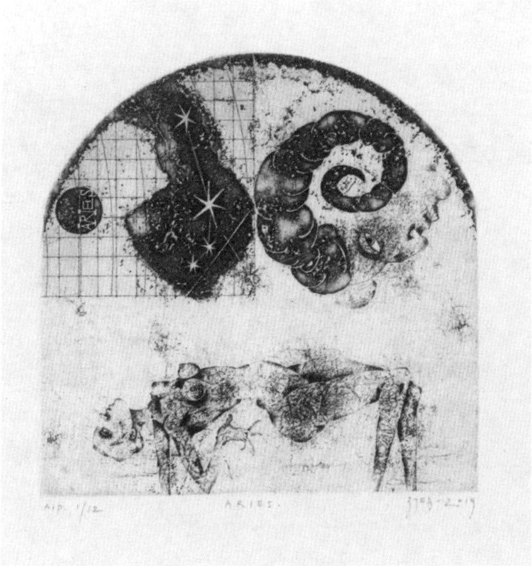

白羊座 / Aries

190

Sit still my heart, do not raise your dust.

Let the world find its way to you.

191

The bow whispers to the arrow before it speeds forth—"Your freedom is mine."

安静坐好，我的心
不要扬起你的风尘
让世界自己去找你

弓对即将离弦的箭低语：
你的自由我做主。

192

Woman, in your laughter you have the music of the fountain of life.

女人，在你的笑声中

音乐如生命之泉涌出

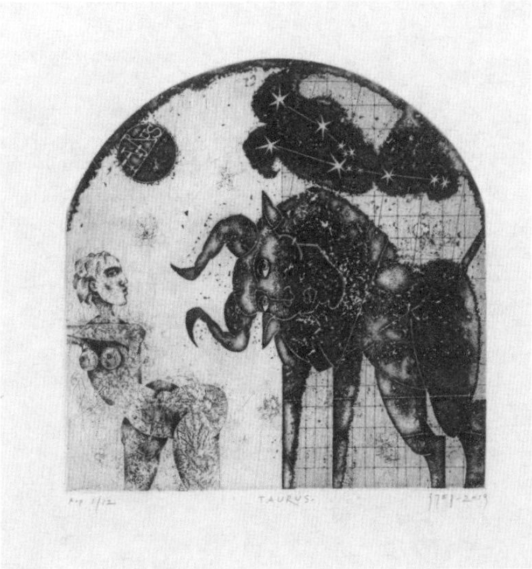

金牛座 / Taurus

193

A mind all logic is like a knife all blade.

It makes the hand bleed that uses it.

194

God loves man's lamp lights better than

his own great stars.

纯粹的逻辑思维

如一把全刃之刀

容易割破手

上帝热爱人间灯火

胜过他自己创造的伟大星光

195

This world is the world of wild storms

kept tame with the music of beauty.

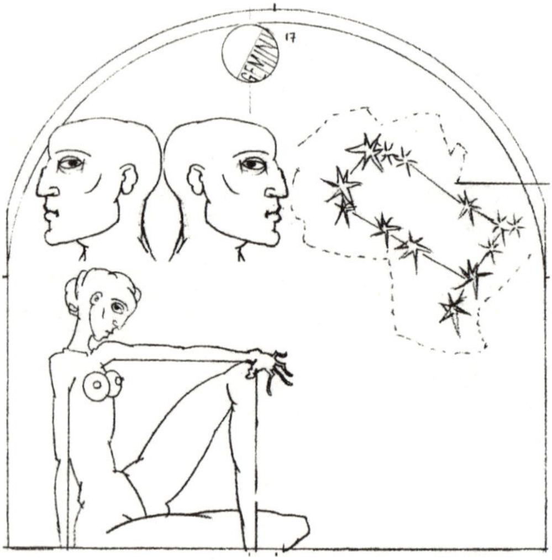

如今的世界曾如疾风骤雨

是美的乐音将它驯服

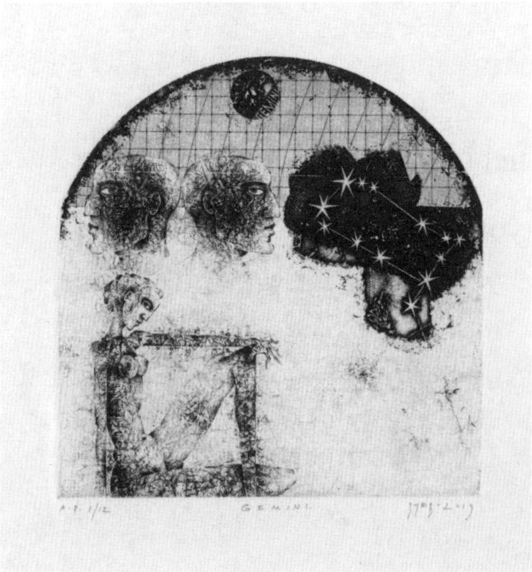

双子座 / Gemini

196

"My heart is like the golden casket of thy kiss," said the sunset cloud to the sun.

197

By touching you may kill, by keeping away you may possess.

“我的心
是一个金色宝盒，
珍藏着你的吻。”
晚霞对太阳说。

远观，你即拥有
亵玩，你就灭亡

198

The cricket's chirp and the patter of rain come to me through the dark, like the rustle of dreams from my past youth.

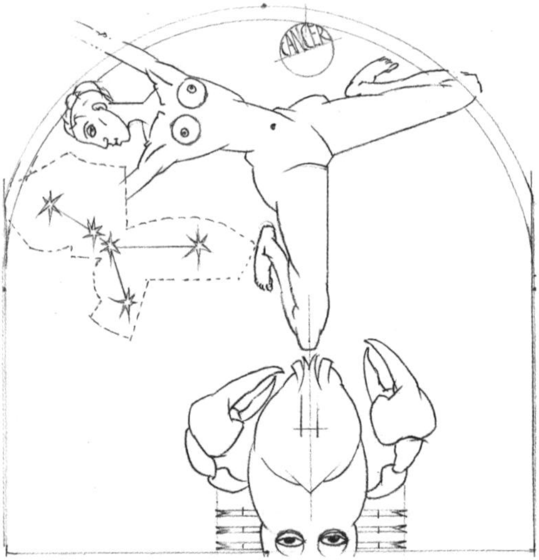

蟋蟀的唧唧声
夜雨的淅沥声
从黑夜传来
犹如逝去的
青春梦呓

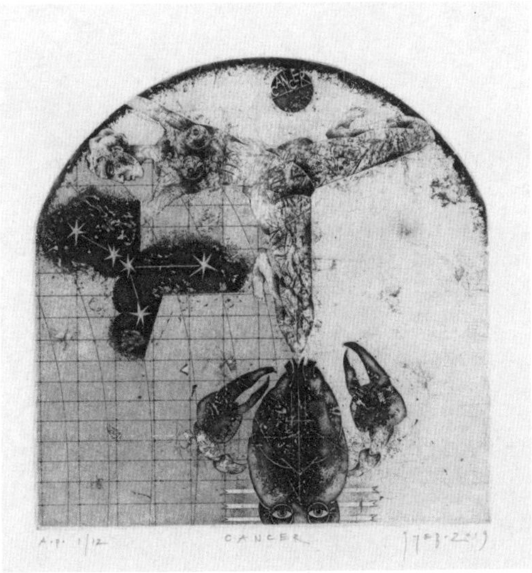

巨蟹座 / Cancer

199

"I have lost my dewdrop," cries the flower to the morning sky that has lost all its stars.

200

The burning log bursts in flame and cries,—"This is my flower, my death."

“我失去了我的露珠，”
鲜花对晨曦哭诉
而晨曦刚刚失去了
它全部的星辰

燃烧的木头
在迸发的火光中大喊：
这就是我的花朵
我的死亡

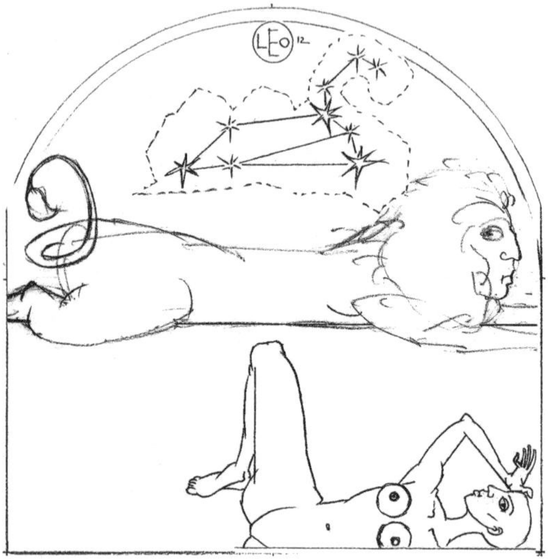
LEO

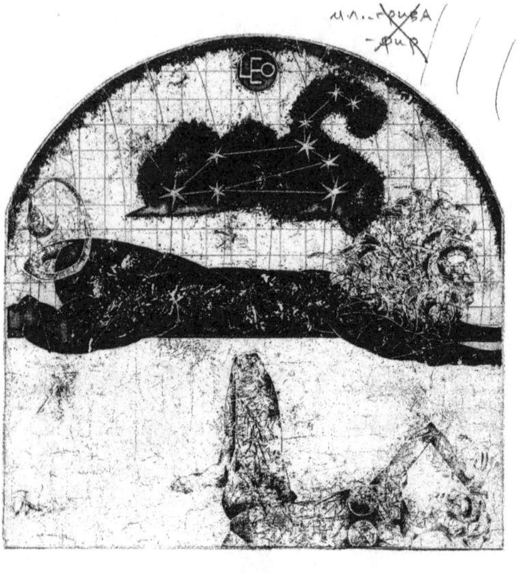
LEO

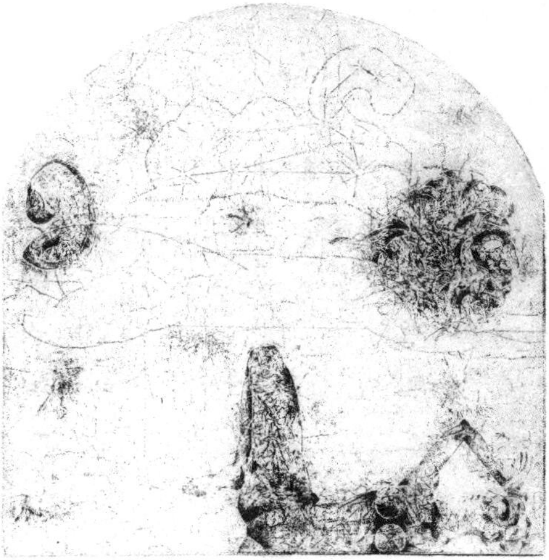

狮子座 / Leo

The wasp thinks that the honey-hive of the neighbouring bees is too small. His neighbours ask him to build one still smaller.

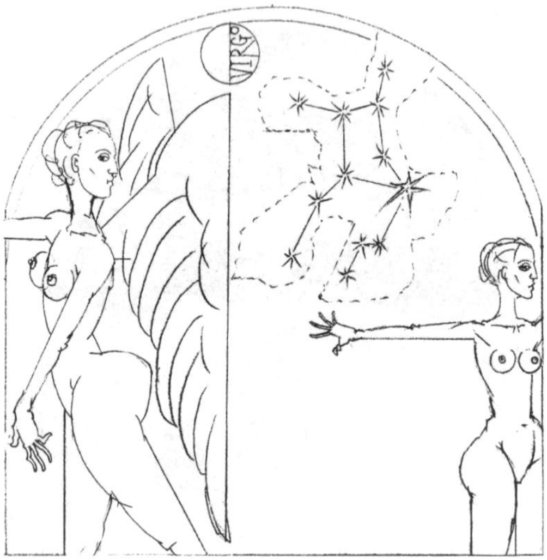

黄蜂觉得隔壁蜜蜂家的巢太小了

可这些邻居还要请他建一个更小的

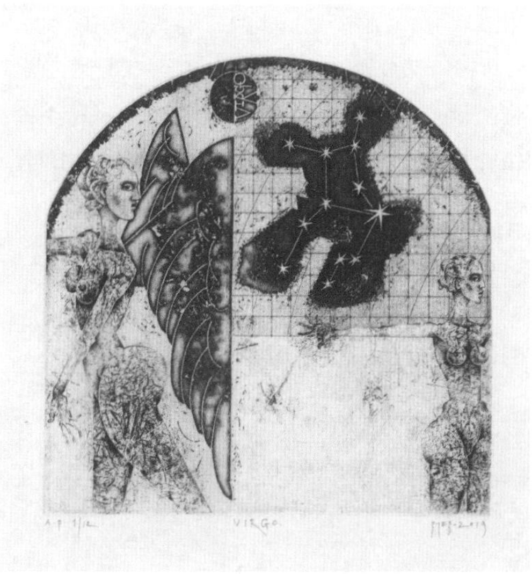

处女座 / Virgo

202

"I cannot keep your waves," says the bank to the river. "Let me keep your footprints in my heart."

203

The day, with the noise of this little earth, drowns the silence of all worlds.

“我无法留住你的波浪，”岸对河说，
“让我在心里留下你的足迹吧。”

白昼用渺小的地球村的喧闹
淹没了茫茫宇宙的沉默

204

The song feels the infinite in the air, the picture in the earth, the poem in the air and the earth; For its words have meaning that walks and music that soars.

歌无垠，在天上

画无垠，在地上

诗无垠，在天地间

因为诗的词句中

有行走大地的意境

有翱翔天宇的音韵

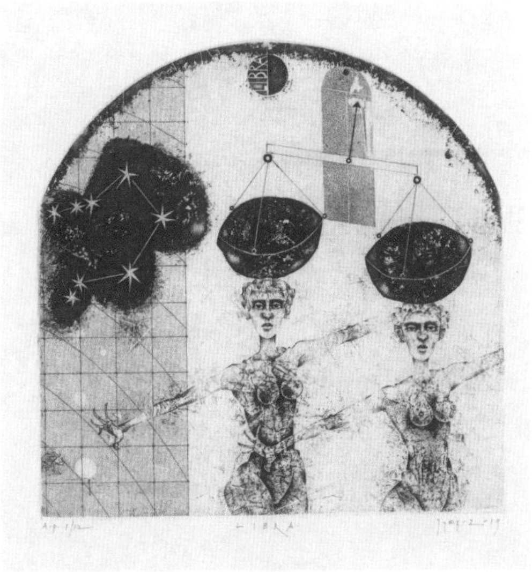

天秤座 / Libra

205

When the sun goes down to the West, the East of his morning stands before him in silence.

206

Let me not put myself wrongly to my world and set it against me.

日薄西山的时候

东方晨辉于夕阳前静立

摆正自己与世界的位置

且勿与自己为敌

Praise shames me, for I secretly beg for it.

赞赏反令我蒙羞

因为我曾私下乞求过它

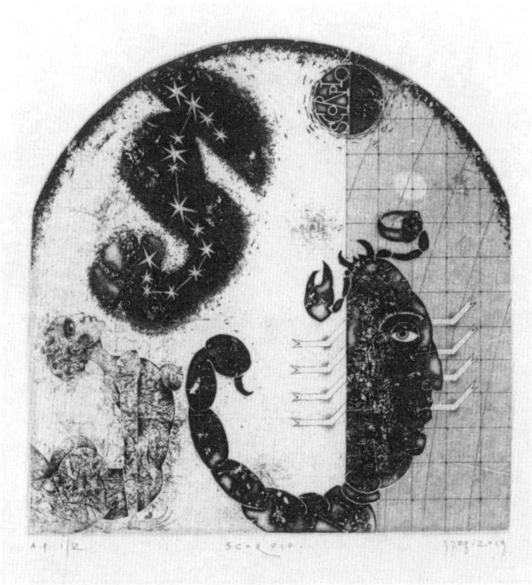

天蝎座 / Scorpio

208

Let my doing nothing when I have nothing to do become untroubled in its depth of peace like the evening in the seashore when the water is silent.

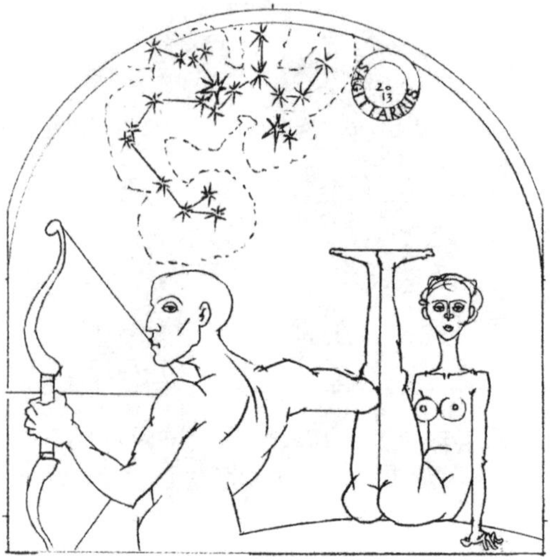

无事可做的时候

就什么也不要做

如风平浪静的海滨之夜

在深度平和中享受从容

射手座 / Sagittarius

209

Maiden, your simplicity, like the blueness of the lake, reveals your depth of truth.

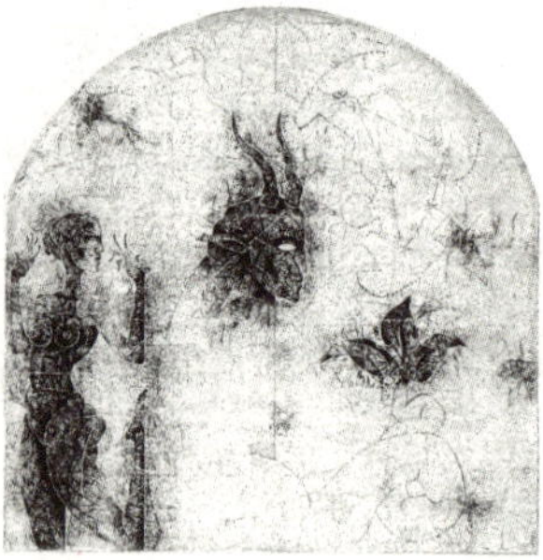

姑娘，你的纯真

如一湖碧水

透出你信仰的深邃

摩羯座 / Capricorn

210

The best does not come alone. It
comes with the company of the all.

211

God's right hand is gentle,
but terrible is his left hand.

最佳者并不特立独行

所有事物均可与之相伴

上帝，右手温柔

其威力在于左手

My evening came among the alien trees
and spoke in a language which my
morning stars did not know.

我的夜晚从一片异域的林中走来

说着一种我的晨星听不懂的语言

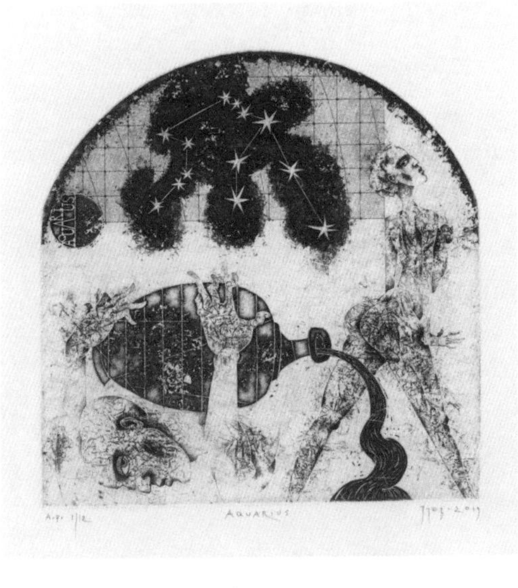

水瓶座 / Aquarius

213

Night's darkness is a bag that bursts with the gold of the dawn.

214

Our desire lends the colours of
the rainbow to the mere mists
and vapours of life.

黑夜是一个口袋

撑满黎明的金光

有了渴盼

原本虚无缥缈的人生

就会变得如彩虹般真实绚烂

215

God waits to win back his own flowers
as gifts from man's hands.

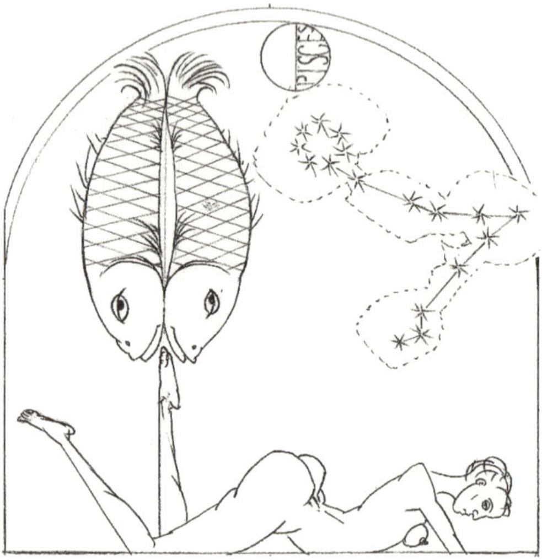

上帝想从人的手里赢回自己的鲜花

他等待人将之作为礼物回赠他

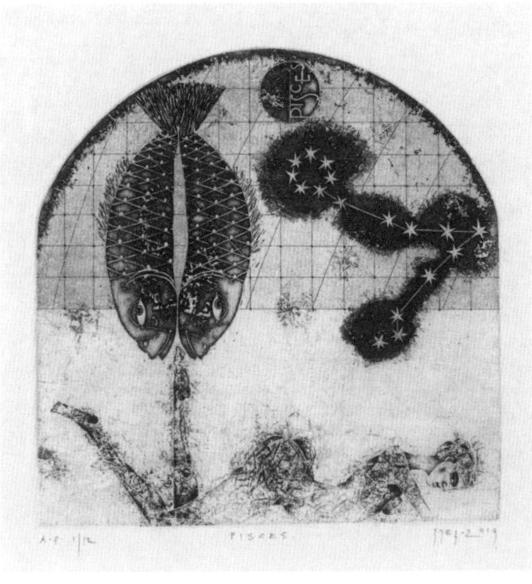

双鱼座 / Pisces

弗拉迪米尔·佐也夫 Vladimir Zuev 俄罗斯艺术家联盟成员，俄罗斯国家职业教育大学（RSVPU）美术系教授，世界公认的铜版画艺术大师。1959 年出生于俄罗斯斯维尔德洛夫斯克地区。1981 年毕业于位于下塔吉尔的国家师范学院美术学院。1986 年至 1991 年多次在莫斯科共和国艺术家之家 Cheliuskinskaya 的版画工作室创作。2010 年荣获俄罗斯荣誉艺术家称号，2012 年因其在文学艺术领域取得的杰出成就获得俄罗斯斯维尔德洛夫斯克州“州长最高荣誉”奖，2014 年荣获俄罗斯艺术学院“伊万·舒瓦洛夫”奖章，2016 年荣获俄罗斯联邦荣誉教育工作者称号。弗拉迪米尔·佐也夫擅长铜版腐蚀法，作品多采用锌版蜡、雕刻和飞尘。参加过 250 多次国际版画艺术展览，获得 70 多个奖项，包括 17 个金奖和 Grand Prix 大奖。在德国、法国、意大利、比利时、丹麦、美国、加拿大、瑞士、日本、捷克、匈牙利、俄罗斯、中国举办过 40 多次个展。

Я с глубокой благодарностью воспринял предложение моих китайских друзей воплотить тему «Зодиак» в серии гравюр.

Концепция серии заключается в том, что три «графических» персонажа: силуэт созвездия, аллегорический символ знака Зодиака и Человек в образе обнаженной женской модели вступают в ритмическо-тональный диалог.

Перед нами – небесный театр актёров, замерших в странных и вместе с тем чувственно-выразительных позах. Тщательно выверенное местоположение каждого «актёра» находится в закономерном подчинении строгой геометрической структуре «небесной сцены».

Владимир Зуев

我非常感谢我的中国朋友提出的以系列版画的形式来表现“十二星座”主题的想法。我这个系列的创作概念来源于三个“图像”特征：星座的轮廓，十二星座的寓意符号以及人类以女性人体模式进入韵调般的对话。我们面前是天穹剧院，里面的演员们被瞬凝在奇特而又同时具有感性表达的姿态中，每个“演员”的精准位置也自然而然地服从“天体”的严格几何结构。

弗拉迪米尔·佐也夫

I am deeply thanked the offer of my Chinese friends to embody the theme of the “Zodiac” in a series of prints.The concept of the series is that three “graphic” characters: the silhouette of the constellation, the allegorical symbol of the zodiac sign and the Human in the image of a naked female model enter into a rhythmic-tonal dialogue.Before us is a celestial theater of actors, which are frozen in strange and at the same time sensual-expressive poses. The carefully calibrated location of each “actor” is naturally subject to the strict geometric structure of the “celestial scene” .

Vladimir Zuev

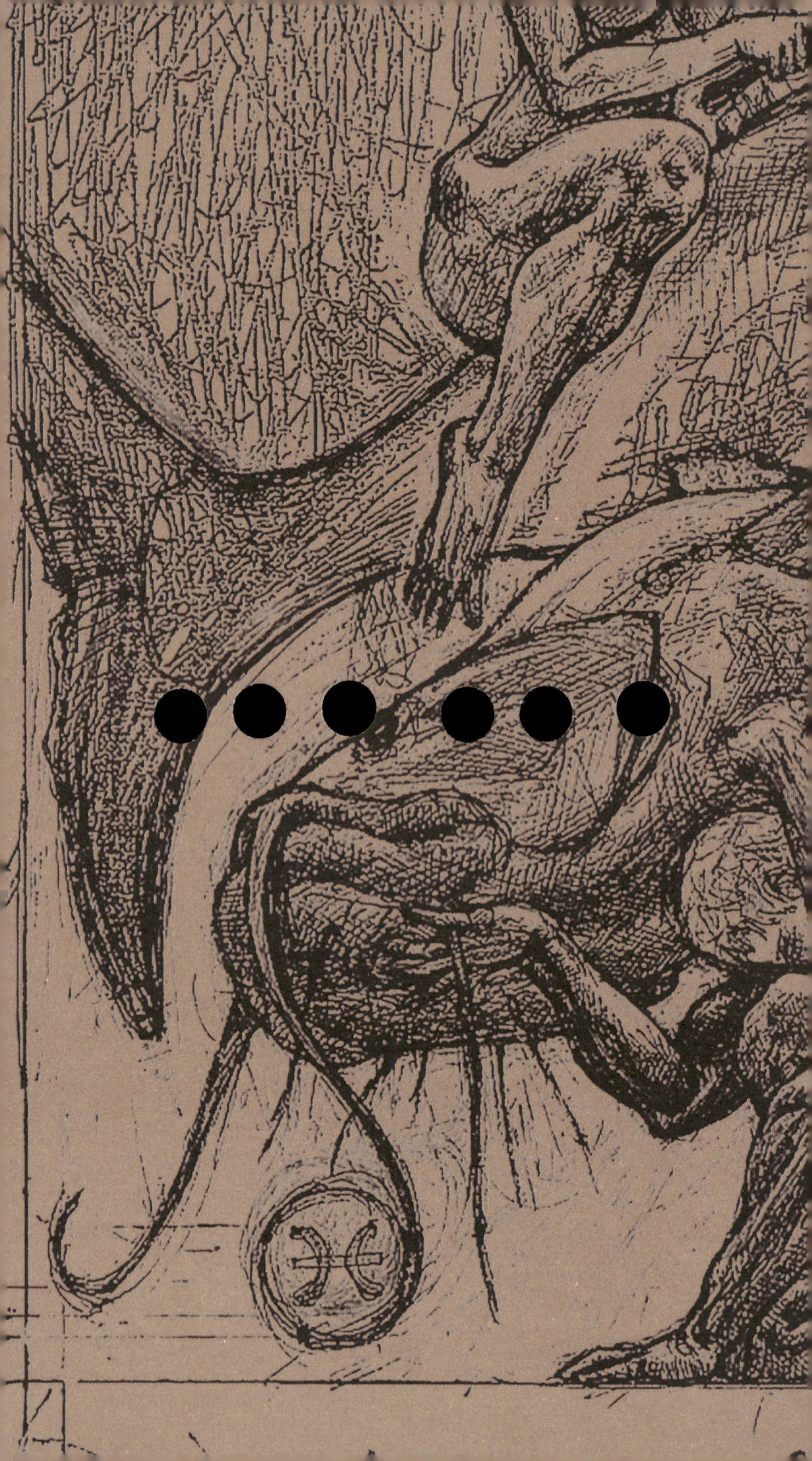

The service of th
fruit is preciou
the service of th
flower is swee

• • • • • •

but let my servic
be the service o
the leaves in i
shade of humb
devotio

216

My sad thoughts tease me asking me their own names.

白羊座 / Aries

悲伤的思绪总是揶揄我

问我它们的名字是什么

金牛座 / Taurus

217

The service of the fruit is precious, the service of the flower is sweet, but let my service be the service of the leaves in its shade of humble devotion.

218

My heart has spread its sails to the idle winds for the shadowy island of Anywhere.

果实的奉献弥足珍贵
鲜花的奉献甜蜜温馨
愿我的奉献如树叶一样谦卑
荫泽大地

我的心在漫不经心的海风中扬帆
驶向那座庇荫的岛屿
无论它地处何方

219

Men are cruel, but Man is kind.

220

Make me thy cup and let my fulness be for thee and for thine.

人本善良

但人类残酷

把我当作您的杯子吧

为您和您的一切斟满

The storm is like the cry of some god in pain whose love the earth refuses.

双子座 / Gemini

暴风雨犹如某位神明痛苦的哭喊

因为大地拒绝了他的爱

巨蟹座 /Cancer

222

The world does not leak because

death is not a crack.

223

Life has become richer by the

love that has been lost.

尘世无处逃遁

因为死亡并非出口

因为失去了爱

生命变得更丰富

224

My friend, your great heart shone with the sunrise of the East like the snowy summit of a lonely hill in the dawn.

225

The fountain of death makes the still water of life play.

我的朋友

你的伟大心灵闪耀着旭日的光辉

仿佛晨曦中孤独的雪山之巅

死亡之泉激活了生命的止水

Those who have everything but thee, my God, laugh at those who have nothing but thyself.

狮子座 / Leo

我的上帝啊

那些无所不有唯独缺少对您信仰的人

居然嘲笑那些一无所有但信仰您的人

处女座 / Virgo

227

The movement of life has its rest

in its own music.

228

Kicks only raise dust and not crops

from the earth.

生命的运动按其自身的音律停歇

踢，只能扬起尘土

而不能从土地上收获庄稼

229

Our names are the light that glows on the sea waves at night and then dies without leaving its signature.

230

Let him only see the thorns who has eyes to see the rose.

我们的名字
只是夜晚海浪发出的微光
转瞬即逝，不留踪迹

让喜爱玫瑰的人
留意一下她的刺

231

Set bird's wings with gold and it will never again soar in the sky.

天秤座 / Libra

给鸟儿的翅膀镶上黄金

它将再也无法翱翔天空

天蝎座 / Scorpio

232

The same lotus of our clime blooms here
in the alien water with the same sweetness,
under another name.

233

In heart's perspective the distance
looms large.

家乡的莲花

在异域的池塘盛开

同样的甜美

却有着不一样的名字

由心观之，疏远令人忧虑

234

The moon has her light all over the sky, her dark spots to herself.

235

Do not say, "It is morning," and dismiss it with a name of yesterday. See it for the first time as a new-born child that has no name.

月亮把光芒全都献给天空
却把黑斑留给自己

不要说："早晨到了"
摒弃这个过时的名词吧
每当初次相见，都把它当作
一个尚未起名的新生儿吧

Smoke boasts to the sky, and Ashes to the earth, that they are brothers to the fire.

射手座 / Sagittarius

烟雾向天空吹嘘

灰烬向大地吹嘘

都自以为是火的兄弟

摩羯座 / Capricorn

237

The raindrop whispered to the jasmine,
"Keep me in your heart for ever."
The jasmine sighed, "Alas," and dropped
to the ground.

238

Timid thoughts, do not be afraid of me.
I am a poet.

雨滴对茉莉低语：

“你要永远记着我”

茉莉“唉”地叹了一口气

跌落在地

胆怯的念头

不必怕我

我是一个诗人

239

The dim silence of my mind seems filled with crickets'chirp—the grey twilight of sound.

240

Rockets, your insult to the stars follows yourself back to the earth.

我阴沉而寂静的思绪中
似乎充斥着蟋蟀窸窣的鸣叫
——那是阴郁的暮色之声

火箭
你冒犯星空
结果跌回地球

241

Thou hast led me through my crowded travels of the day to my evening's loneliness.
I wait for its meaning through the stillness of the night.

水瓶座 / Aquarius

您引领我从日出而作的繁忙
来到日落而息的孤独
透过夜的宁静
我等待领悟
孤独的含义

双鱼座 /Pisces

242

This life is the crossing of a sea, where
we meet in the same narrow ship.
In death we reach the shore and go to
our different worlds.

243

The stream of truth flows through its
channels of mistakes.

今生，犹如渡海
我们相逢于同一叶扁舟
死时，我们抵岸
各奔不同的来世

真理的溪流
常常会穿过
谬误的沟渠

朱利安·乔丹诺夫 Julian Jordanov 当代保加利亚版画界的代表艺术家，世界级版画艺术家。1965年出生于保加利亚洛维奇。1995年毕业于保加利亚索菲亚国家美术学院，美术学硕士。第一、二、三届瓦尔纳国际版画藏书票大赛艺术总监。擅长铜版和石版，尤其是腐蚀和飞尘技法。作品强调力量感、气场感、其创作主题多为表现圣经故事、神话故事。在保加利亚、德国、白俄罗斯、土耳其、比利时和中国等国家举办过超过30次个展。他的作品屡获盛誉，参加过60余次国际展览和比赛，并获包含一等奖、大师荣誉奖等在内的20多个奖项，包括比利时国际藏书票展凹版技法特别奖；土耳其安卡拉第一届国际藏书票大赛一等奖；第32届北京国际版画藏书票双年展金奖；保加利亚第二届国际藏书票双年展保加利亚藏书票奖；第一届国际藏书票和小版画双年展提名奖等。

Проектът „Зодиакални знаци" е великолепна идея, хвърляща мост между различните култури със своя универсален характер, даващ същевременно възможност за съвсем специфична интерпретация на символиката.
За мен е чест и голямо удоволствие да бъда част от това събитие, наред с толкова значими имена в съвременната графика – художници с голям талант, висок професионализъм и уникален поглед върху заобикалящия ни свят.

J. Jordanov

The project "Zodiac Signs" is a magnificent idea which is building the bridge between different cultures with it's multipurpose nature, giving at the same time possibilities for individual interpretation of the symbols. For me is a big pleasure and honor to be part of this event together with such important names of contemporary graphic artists with great talent, high professional skills and unique point of view at the surrounding World.

Julian Jordanov

"星迹"项目是一个杰出的想法，它以其多向性在不同文化之间架起了一座桥梁，同时也为个体解释这些符号提供了可能性。对我来说，能够与世界上这些才华横溢、技艺高超、观点独特，有着重要声誉的当代著名版画艺术家一同参与这次盛会，是无上的快乐与巨大的荣幸。

朱利安·乔丹诺夫

"How may

sing to the

and worship,

Sun?" asked th

little flowe

"By the simpl

silence of th

purity," answere

the sur

244

My heart is homesick to-day for the one sweet hour across the sea of time.

白羊座 / Aries

今天我的心中充满乡愁

为跨越时间之海的甜蜜时刻

金牛座 / Taurus

245

The bird-song is the echo of the morning light back from the earth.

246

"Are you too proud to kiss me?" the morning light asks the buttercup.

鸟儿的鸣唱

是晨曦从大地反馈的回声

“你如此傲慢，不屑于吻我吗？ ”

晨曦问毛茛

247

"How may I sing to thee and worship, O Sun?" asked the little flower.
"By the simple silence of thy purity," answered the sun.

248

Man is worse than an animal
when he is an animal.

“哦，太阳！
我该如何向您歌唱和膜拜啊？”
小花问道。
“用你的纯真和缄默即可。”
太阳答道。

当人沦为禽兽
禽兽不如

249

Dark clouds become heaven's flowers when kissed by light.

双子座 / Gemini

乌云被光明亲吻

变身天堂的花朵

巨蟹座 / Cancer

250

Let not the sword-blade mock its handle for being blunt.

251

The night's silence, like a deep lamp, is burning with the light of its milky way.

剑刃莫要嘲笑剑柄的粗钝

夜的寂静
如一盏深邃的灯
燃烧着银河的光芒

252

Around the sunny island of Life swells day and night death's limitless song of the sea.

253

Is not this mountain like a flower, with its petals of hills, drinking the sunlight?

生命之岛

充满阳光

环绕的大海却日夜澎湃着

无穷无尽的死亡之歌

这座山

不像一朵花吗

山峦是它的花瓣

阳光是它的甘露

254

The real with its meaning read wrong

and emphasis misplaced is the unreal.

狮子座 / Leo

真实

如果其义被误读，本末被倒置

即为不真实

处女座 / Virgo

255

Find your beauty, my heart, from the world's movement, like the boat that has the grace of the wind and the water.

256

The eyes are not proud of their sight but of their eyeglasses.

我的心啊

从世事变迁中发现你的美吧

如同船的优雅来自风和浪

眼睛以眼镜为荣

而非视力

257

I live in this little world of mine and am afraid to make it the least less.
Lift me into thy world and let me have the freedom gladly to lose my all.

258

The false can never grow into truth by growing in power.

我生活在自我的渺小世界里

依然患得患失

请把我提升到您的境界

放弃一切，乐享自由

谬误，永远不会因其力量的增长

而成为真理

My heart, with its lapping waves of song, longs to caress this green world of the sunny day.

天秤座 / Libra

我的心，和着海浪拍击的音乐

渴望抚摸阳光明媚的绿色世界

天蝎座 / Scorpio

260

Wayside grass, love the star, then your dreams will come out in flowers.

261

Let your music, like a sword, pierce the noise of the market to its heart.

路边的小草
去爱星星吧
那样你的梦想
就会在花丛中盛开

让你的音乐
如一把利剑
刺透市井的喧闹
直抵市井的心窝

262

The trembling leaves of this tree touch my heart like the fingers of an infant child.

263

The sadness of my soul is her bride's veil. It waits to be lifted in the night.

这棵树上

摇曳的树叶

如婴儿的手指

触摸我的心房

我灵魂的悲伤犹如新娘的面纱[①]

要等到夜晚方能摘下

①：英文原版即与第 98 首相同

The little flower lies in the dust.

It sought the path of the butterfly.

射手座 / Sagittarius

落于尘土的小花

找寻蝴蝶经过的小径

摩羯座 / Capricorn

265

I am in the world of the roads. The night comes. Open thy gate, thou world of the home.

266

I have sung the songs of thy day. In the evening let me carry thy lamp through the stormy path.

我身处“路”的世界

夜晚来临

请打开您的大门

我要回到“家”的世界

唱完你那个时代的歌曲

入夜，让我提着你的灯

穿过那风雨交加的小径

267

I do not ask thee into the house.
Come into my infinite loneliness, my
Lover.

268

Death belongs to life as birth does.
The walk is in the raising of the foot
as in the laying of it down.

我的爱人

我请求你进入的不是这所房子

而是我无尽的孤独

生与死都是生命题中应有之义

如抬步、落步都属于行走一样

269

I have learnt the simple meaning of thy whispers in flowers and sunshine—teach me to know thy words in pain and death.

水瓶座 / Aquarius

我已领悟了你在鲜花和阳光中低语的真义

请教导我理解你关于痛苦和死亡的箴言吧

双鱼座 / Pisces

It was a great honor and pleasure for me to create 12 graphics inspired by a theme that has always excited me. I live in a place where the ancient Thracian tradition in art is deeply connected with Greek aesthetics and mythology. This formed my view of the subject, and I remained faithful to our mythological notions of the constellations and the zodiac. Many thanks to the organizers for this unique opportunity.

Hristo Naidenov

对我来说，能以这个激发灵感的主题创作这 12 幅作品是我的荣幸。我所居住的地方，融合了色雷斯人古老的艺术传统和希腊美学与神话观念，这构建了我对该主题的视角。我的创作遵从了星座和黄道十二宫的神话观念。非常感谢这次难得的机会。

赫里斯托 · 奈德诺夫

赫里斯托·奈德诺夫　Hristo Naidenov　保加利亚著名版画家，保加利亚大特尔诺沃大学艺术博士、副教授。1971 年出生于保加利亚上奥里亚霍维察市。1994 年至 1999 年就读于大特尔诺沃大学版画专业，师从尼古拉·哈吉塔涅夫教授。2000 年起在大特尔诺沃大学美术系任版画专业副教授，2016 年获博士学位。创作领域主要为微缩雕刻、插图和版画藏书票。喜欢创作的主题有神话，古代文化，文学和诗歌。常用的技术：运用蚀刻、干刻、飞尘、美柔汀等铜版画的综合技法，刻版精细，营造出梦幻与现实的意境。在 20 多次国际赛事上荣获各种奖项，包括 2004 年日本东京举行的日本版画藏书票协会第 15 届新湖畔大赛一等奖；2016 年保加利亚瓦尔纳举行的第二届国际版画藏书票大赛爱德华·潘科夫特别奖；2018 年捷克布拉格举行的第 37 届国际版画藏书票双年展荣誉奖等。作品被来自美国、澳大利亚、法国、意大利、德国、荷兰、英国、比利时、日本、加拿大、中国和保加利亚的艺术机构和私人收藏。

Zodiak je po staletí velkou
uměleckou inspirací.
Cílem mé grafické tvorby
je dát každému z jeho znamení
současnou tvář.

Vlad Suchánek

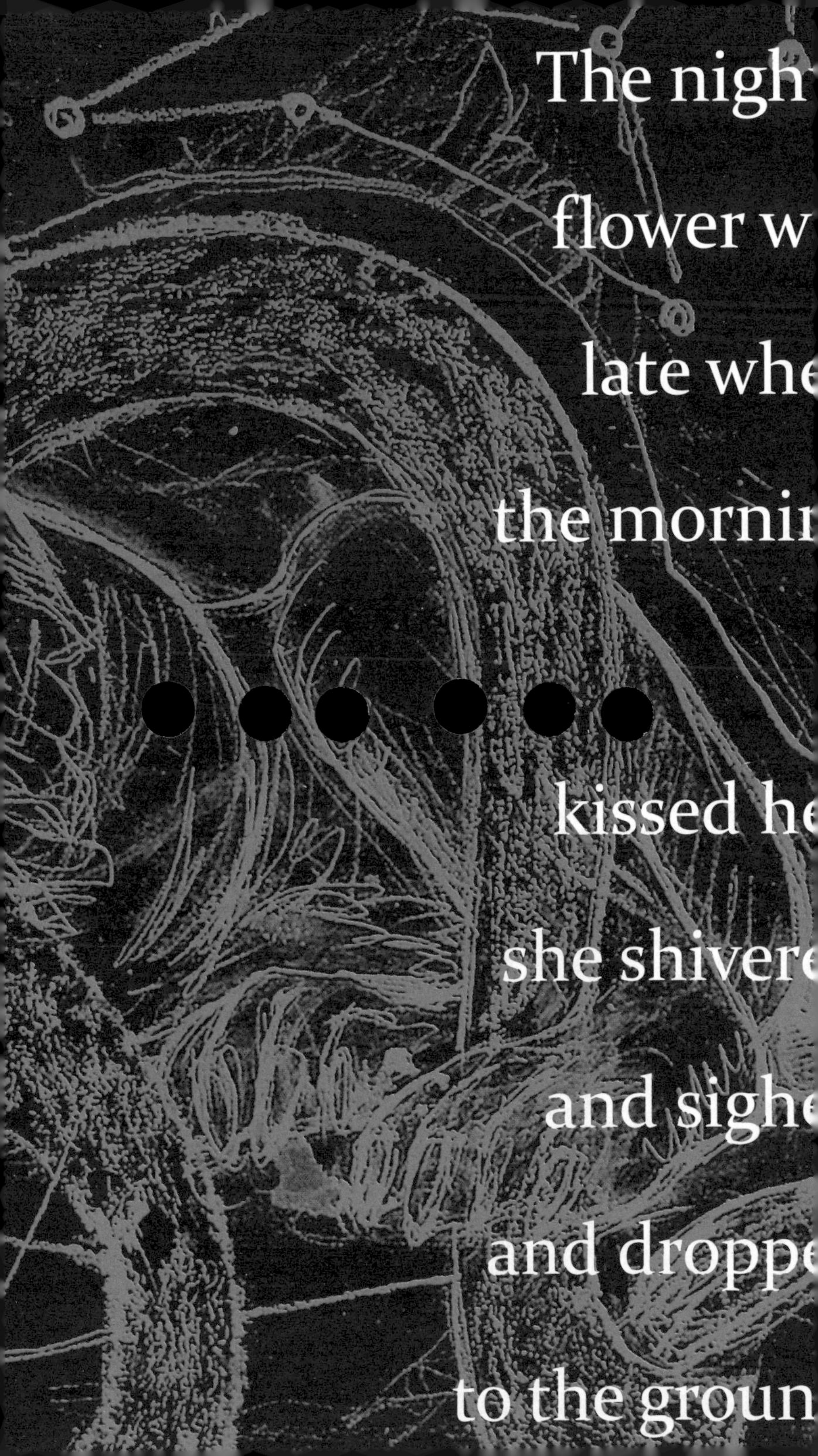

The nigh

flower w

late whe

the mornin

kissed he

she shivere

and sighe

and droppe

to the groun

270

The night's flower was late when the morning kissed her, she shivered and sighed and dropped to the ground.

白羊座 / Aries

当清晨去吻她的时候

夜之花姗姗来迟

她战栗着

叹息着

飘落到

地上

金牛座 / Taurus

271

Through the sadness of all things
I hear the crooning of the Eternal
Mother.

272

I came to your shore as a stranger, I lived
in your house as a guest, I leave your door
as a friend, my earth.

透过万物的悲伤

我听到永恒之母的低吟

大地啊

登陆你的岸时，我是个陌生人

住到你的房里时，我是个客人

离你而去时，我成了你的朋友

273

Let my thoughts come to you, when I am gone, like the afterglow of sunset at the margin of starry silence.

274

Light in my heart the evening star of rest and then let the night whisper to me of love.

当我离开时

让我的思想来到你身边

如落日余晖洒在静谧星空的边缘

请在我心中点燃伴我安眠的夜星

然后，让夜向我倾诉衷肠

275

I am a child in the dark. I stretch my hands through the coverlet of night for thee, Mother.

双子座 / Gemini

我是黑暗中的一个孩子

我从夜的被单中伸出手找您，妈妈

巨蟹座 / Cancer

276

The day of work is done. Hide my face
in your arms, Mother.
Let me dream.

277

The lamp of meeting burns long; it goes
out in a moment at the parting.

一天的活儿干完了

妈妈，请把我的脸藏进你的臂弯

让我进入梦乡

灯，为相聚长明

为分别熄灭

278

One word keep for me in thy silence, O World, when I am dead, "I have loved."

279

We live in this world when we love it.

哦，世界
当我死的时候
请您默默地为我留存一句话
我爱过

我们爱这个世界
才活在这个世界

Let the dead have the immortality of fame,

but the living the immortality of love.

狮子座 / Leo

愿逝者名垂千古

愿生者永沐爱河

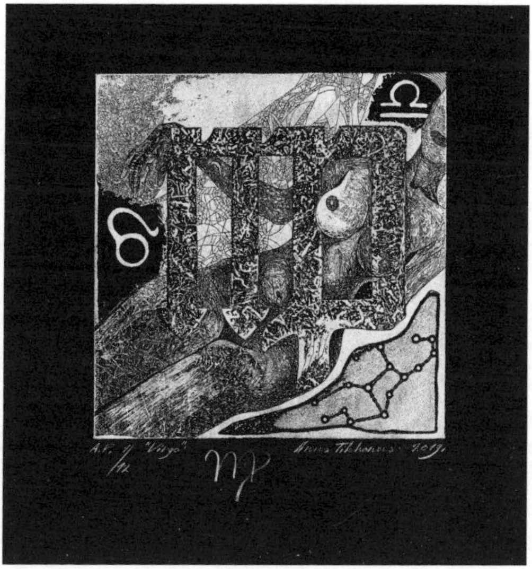

处女座 / Virgo

281

I have seen thee as the half-awakened child sees his mother in the dusk of the dawn and then smiles and sleeps again.

282

I shall die again and again to know that life is inexhaustible.

我见到您

就像一个半梦半醒的孩子

在黎明的曙光中见到妈妈

笑笑，又睡去

我将一次又一次死去

以知晓生命没有穷尽

283

While I was passing with the crowd in the road I saw thy smile from the balcony and I sang and forgot all noise.

284

Love is life in its fullness like the cup with its wine.

路上，我随波逐流

忽然，瞥见阳台上你的微笑

我放声歌唱，忘掉了喧嚣

爱让生命饱满

如酒杯斟满佳酿

285

They light their own lamps and sing their own words in their temples.
But the birds sing thy name in thine own morning light,—for thy name is joy.

天秤座 / Libra

他们在自己的庙宇里
点燃自己的灯
唱响自己的歌
但鸟儿们在您的晨光里
咏唱您的名字
——因为您的名字就是快乐

天蝎座 / Scorpio

286

Lead me in the centre of thy silence
to fill my heart with songs.

287

Let them live who choose in their own
hissing world of fireworks.
My heart longs for thy stars, my God.

领我进入你沉默的中心
用歌声充实我的心

就让他们生活在他们自己选择的
嘈杂的烟花世界吧
我的上帝啊，我的内心向往您的星空

288

Love's pain sang round my life like the unplumbed sea, and love's joy sang like birds in its flowering groves.

289

Put out the lamp when thou wishest. I shall know thy darkness and shall love it.

爱的痛苦
如深不可测的大海
围绕着我的生命歌唱
而爱的欢愉
如鸟儿在繁花丛中放歌

许愿的时候
请熄灭灯光
我懂你的黑暗并爱它

290

When I stand before thee at the day's end thou shalt see my scars and know that I had my wounds and also my healing.

射手座 / Sagittarius

最终

当我站在你的面前

你将看到我的伤疤

你将知道我受过伤

且已愈合

摩羯座 / Capricorn

291

Some day I shall sing to thee in the sunrise of some other world, "I have seen thee before in the light of the earth, in the love of man."

292

Clouds come floating into my life from other days no longer to shed rain or usher storm but to give colour to my sunset sky.

有朝一日
在某个来世的旭日朝霞中
我会对你歌唱：
我曾在地球的光芒中
在人类的爱中
见过你

昔日的浮云
飘进我的生活
不再呼风唤雨
只是给我落日的天空
添一抹色彩

293

Truth raises against itself the storm
that scatters its seeds broadcast.

294

The storm of the last night has
crowned this morning with golden
peace.

真理引发了反对自己的风暴
但风暴却把真理的种子播撒天下

昨夜的风暴
用金色的和平
为今晨加冕

295

Truth seems to come with its final word;

and the final word gives birth to its next.

水瓶座 / Aquarius

真理似乎总与定论相伴

而定论又会产生新的结论

双鱼座 / Pisces

安娜·缇科诺娃 Anna Tikhonova 白俄罗斯现代美术馆科学研究和展览部门负责人、版画藏书票收藏馆馆长，白俄罗斯美术家联盟和白俄罗斯作家联盟的会员。1977 年生于白俄罗斯明斯克。1996 年至 2002 年就读于明斯克的白俄罗斯国家艺术学院版画系；2004 年至 2007 年就读于白俄罗斯国家艺术学院美术史与理论系获硕士学位；著有20世纪到21世纪初白俄罗斯和欧洲版画藏书票科学研究刊物。从 1997 年起开始在白俄罗斯和国际上举办过 9 次个展，数十次群展和比赛，并荣获 18 次国际奖项，包括 2005 年比利时圣尼古拉斯第 15 届版画藏书票双年展凹版一等奖，2015 年德国 DEG 大会版画藏书票展一等奖等。艺术作品被白俄罗斯现代美术博物馆、奥地利国家图书馆、比利时国际版画藏书票中心、伊斯坦布尔版画藏书票博物馆、保加利亚瓦尔纳版画艺术馆，以及白俄罗斯、俄罗斯、乌克兰、立陶宛、波兰、德国、奥地利、比利时、荷兰、保加利亚、捷克、斯洛伐克、土耳其、意大利、西班牙、瑞士、希腊、日本、中国、美国、澳大利亚等国的私人机构所收藏和展览。

能与其他国家的杰出艺术家朋友们一起参与星座项目是我的荣幸，也是一项艰巨的责任，因为我是十二位艺术家中唯一的女性。

安娜·缇科诺娃

It is a big honor for me to be a participant of the "Zodiac" project together with outstanding graphic colleagues from different countries and also a big responsibility, because I am the only female from the 12 artists.

Anna Tikhonova

Для мяне вялікі гонар быць удзельніцай праекту "Задыяк" разам з выбітнымі калегамі-графікамі з іншых краін і таксама вялікая адказнасць, бо я адзіная жанчына з 12 мастакоў.

Hanna Tsikhanava
(Anna Tikhonova)

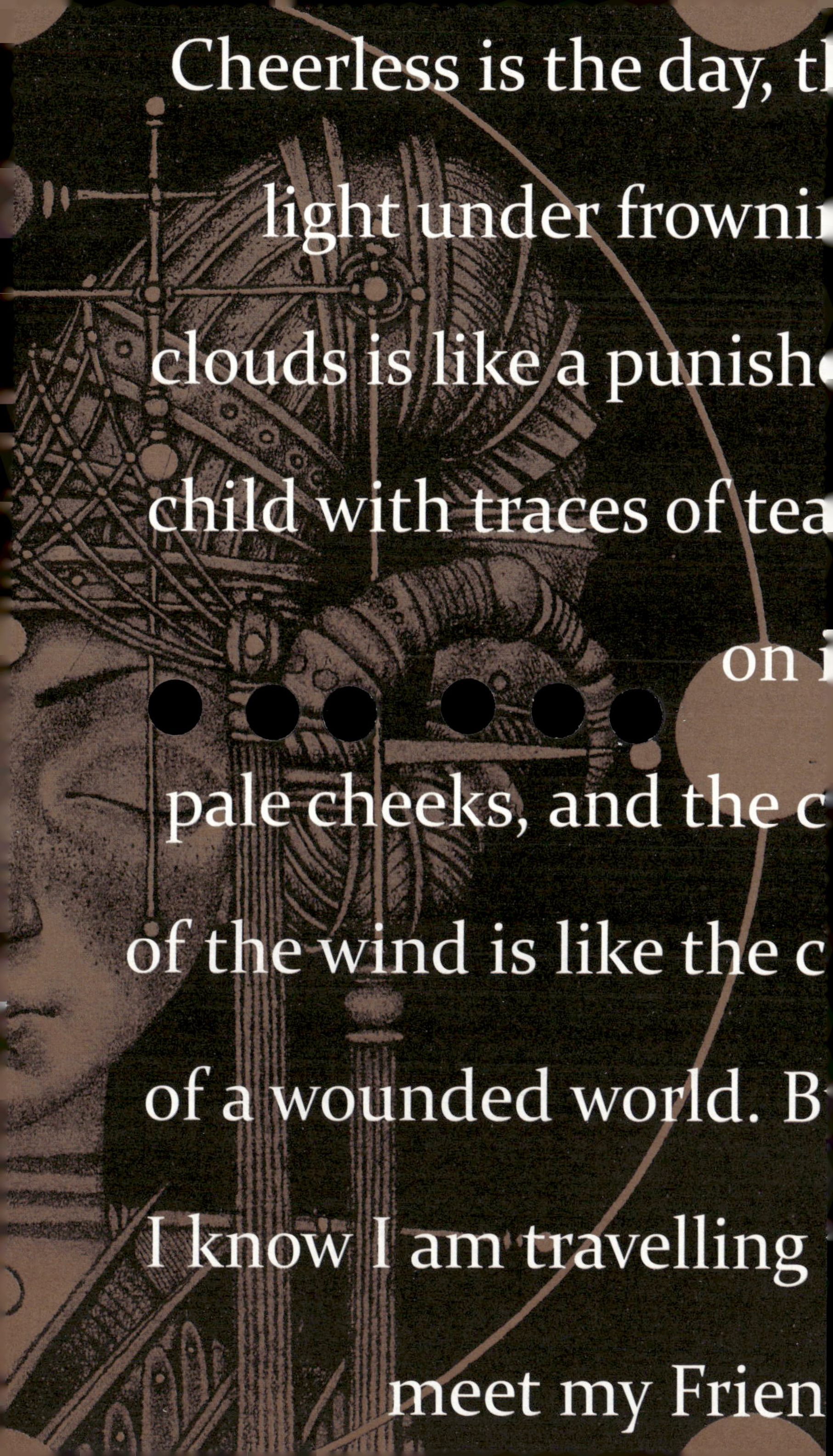

Cheerless is the day, t

light under frowni

clouds is like a punish

child with traces of tea

on

pale cheeks, and the c

of the wind is like the c

of a wounded world. B

I know I am travelling

meet my Frien

296

Blessed is he whose fame does

not outshine his truth.

白羊座 / Aries

名副其实的人好福气

金牛座 / Taurus

297

Sweetness of thy name fills my heart when I forget mine—like thy morning sun when the mist is melted.

298

The silent night has the beauty of the mother and the clamorous day of the child.

当我忘掉自己的名字
你的名字就占据我的心室
如此甜蜜，宛若
雾散时分的朝阳

寂静的夜晚蕴含母性之美
喧闹的白天彰显少年之美

299

The world loved man when he smiled. The world became afraid of him when he laughed.

300

God waits for man to regain his childhood in wisdom.

微笑赢得爱意

大笑引发恐惧

上帝期待

人在智慧中重获童真

301

Let me feel this world as thy love taking form, then my love will help it.

双子座 / Gemini

你的爱造就了这个世界
让我好好感受，然后
我也把爱献给它

巨蟹座 / Cancer

302

Thy sunshine smiles upon the winter days of my heart, never doubting of its spring flowers.

303

God kisses the finite in his love and man the infinite.

你的阳光
在我内心的严冬里微笑
它对春暖花开深信不疑

上帝用爱亲吻有限
人则用爱亲吻无限

304

Thou crossest desert lands of barren years
to reach the moment of fulfilment.

305

God's silence ripens man's
thoughts into speech.

历经多年的沙漠跋涉
你终于到达功成圆满的时刻

上帝的沉默催熟人的思想
使之成为言语

306

Thou wilt find, Eternal Traveller, marks
of thy footsteps across my songs.

狮子座 / Leo

永恒的行者

你将发现，你的足迹遍布我的歌

处女座 / Virgo

307

Let me not shame thee, Father, who displayest thy glory in thy children.

308

Cheerless is the day, the light under frowning clouds is like a punished child with traces of tears on its pale cheeks, and the cry of the wind is like the cry of a wounded world. But I know I am travelling to meet my Friend.

天父，您的荣耀光照子孙

我不会令您蒙羞

愁云遮日

这阴郁的日子像

一个受罚的孩子

苍白的脸颊上挂着泪痕

风的呼号

如伤痕累累的世界

在哭喊

但我知道

我正在行进

去见我的朋友

309

To-night there is a stir among the palm leaves, a swell in the sea, Full Moon, like the heart throb of the world. From what unknown sky hast thou carried in thy silence the aching secret of love?

310

I dream of a star, an island of light, where I shall be born and in the depth of its quickening leisure my life will ripen its works like the ricefield in the autumn sun.

今夜
棕榈叶婆娑作响
大海波涛汹涌
“满月”如同世界的心悸
你默默地
从哪一片未知的天空
带来爱的痛苦和神秘

我梦见一颗星
一座光芒的岛屿
我应该在那里出生
并沉浸于极度的闲适
我的生命将催熟我的作品
如同秋天的太阳催熟稻田

311

The smell of the wet earth in the rain rises like a great chant of praise from the voiceless multitude of the insignificant.

312

That love can ever lose is a fact that we cannot accept as truth.

雨中，泥土的芬芳弥漫着
仿佛是那些默默无闻的
卑微大众发出的伟大赞歌

爱会失去，这个事实
我们无法接受为真理

313

We shall know some day that death can never rob us of that which our soul has gained, for her gains are one with herself.

天秤座 / Libra

总有一天，我们会明白

死亡永远不会掠走我们灵魂的收获

因为灵魂的收获就是灵魂本身

天蝎座 / Scorpio

314

God comes to me in the dusk of my evening with the flowers from my past kept fresh in his basket.

315

When all the strings of my life will be tuned, my Master, then at every touch of thine will come out the music of love.

上帝在暮色中
向我走来
我昔日的鲜花
在他的提篮里
鲜艳如初

我的主啊
当我生命中所有的琴弦
都被调准
您的每一次弹拨
都会产生爱的乐音

316

Let me live truly, my Lord,

so that death to me become true.

317

Man's history is waiting in patience for

the triumph of the insulted man.

主啊，让我真实地活着
那样，死亡对我也就变得真实了

人类的历史
正在耐心地等待
被侮辱者的胜利

318

I feel thy gaze upon my heart this moment like the sunny silence of the morning upon the lonely field whose harvest is over.

射手座 / Sagittarius

此刻，我感到你的目光

落在我的心上

如同清晨寂静的阳光

落在收割之后孤独的田野上

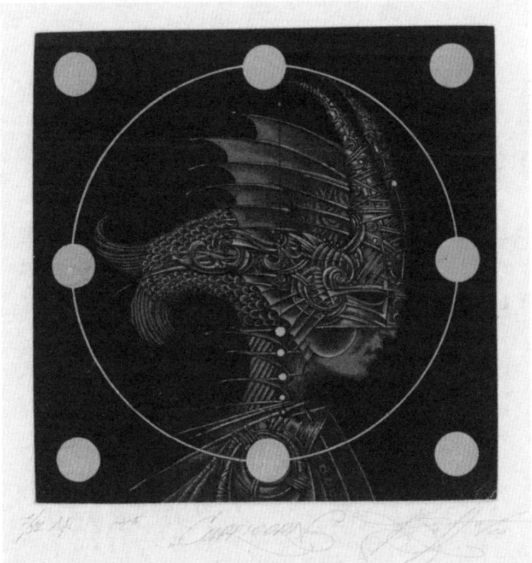

摩羯座 / Capricorn

319

I long for the Island of Songs across this heaving Sea of Shouts.

320

The prelude of the night is commenced in the music of the sunset, in its solemn hymn to the ineffable dark.

跨越波涛起伏的喧嚣之海
我渴望歌声之岛

夜的序幕
始于落日的乐章
始于对不可言状的黑暗的庄严
赞美

321

I have scaled the peak and found no shelter in fame's bleak and barren height. Lead me, my Guide, before the light fades, into the valley of quiet where life's harvest mellows into golden wisdom.

322

Things look phantastic in this dimness of the dusk—the spires whose bases are lost in the dark and tree tops like blots of ink. I shall wait for the morning and wake up to see thy city in the light.

我曾经登顶

但荒芜的荣誉之巅

无处栖身，高处不胜寒

向导啊，请引领我

在光明消失之前，进入寂静的山谷

在那里，人生的收获将逐渐成熟

变成金色的智慧

黯淡的暮色

令万物出现离奇的幻影

黑暗中

尖塔失去了塔基

树冠墨迹斑斑

我要等到清晨，醒来

在光明中一睹你的城池

323

I have suffered and despaired and known death and I am glad that I am in this great world.

水瓶座 / Aquarius

经历了苦难

经历了绝望

懂得了死亡

我庆幸我生活在

这个伟大的世界

双鱼座 / Pisces

324

There are tracts in my life that are bare and silent. They are the open spaces where my busy days had their light and air.

325

Release me from my unfulfilled past clinging to me from behind making death difficult.

我生命中有
大片的荒凉和静寂
在这些空旷之地
我匆忙的时光获得了
光明和空气

往昔
壮志未酬
此情
挥之不去
念之
死不瞑目
请帮我从中解脱吧

326

Let this be my last word,

that I trust in thy love.

这就是我的遗言：

我笃信你的爱

亲爱的晓庄，感谢你的来信。我将在 11 月寄出我的作品。接下来几个月我将努力完成画作的框架。画作完成时我会及时通知你。现在我在去往深圳观澜美术馆的途中，去参加 Jochen Kublik 画展的开幕式。星迹将会是一个宏大而卓越的项目。有这么多了不起的艺术家都会参与其中。能与他们为伍是我的荣幸。我将为此竭尽所能。

在德国向你祝好！

罗曼 · 萨斯托夫

罗曼·萨斯托夫 Roman Sustov　白俄罗斯美术家协会会员，白俄罗斯著名艺术家。1977 年出生于白俄罗斯明斯克。1995 年毕业于明斯克艺术学院。2001 年毕业于白俄罗斯国家艺术学院版画系。2001 年至 2005 年就职于白俄罗斯文化部艺术绘画工作室。2005 年加入白俄罗斯美术家协会版画部。2013 年起在白俄罗斯国家艺术学院版画系任教，并获硕士学位。罗曼·萨斯托夫一直从事版画和书籍插图的创作。多次参加国内外的版画展和比赛，获得奖项证书不计其数。多件作品被美国、德国、荷兰、波兰、乌克兰、日本、俄罗斯及白俄罗斯等国的公共美术馆和私人收藏馆收藏。版画藏书票在艺术家的创作中占有特殊的位置。至今，已经为世界各地的知名收藏家定制创作了 120 余件版画藏书票作品，作品备受版画收藏家们的青睐。其在书籍设计方面同样见长，与俄罗斯、白俄罗斯等国的多家出版社合作，共创作插图书籍多达 20 余本，自 1999 年以来在“一位艺术家一本书”展览大赛中多次获胜。他在油画和邮票设计领域同样硕果累累，还是一名出色的舞美师和服装设计师。

Dear Xiaozhuang,Thank you very much for your message! I will send the works in November. I will try to finish my sketches in the coming months. I will let you know when it is ready.Now I'm on my way to Shenzhen and Guanlan museum for the opening of a group exhibition curated by Jochen Kublik.Now I can see that it is going to be a very big and remarkable project!So many great artists are involved in it.Dusan Kallay is one of my favorite artists in printmaking. It is pleasure to in such company. I'll try to do my best for this project!Best regards from Germany

Roman